IN IT FOR THE LONG HAUL

Making the Most of working remotely in the resources sector

3RD EDITION

JOHN TOOMEY

In it for the Long Haul

"Making the Most of working remotely in the Resources Sector."
3rd Edition

In it for the Long Haul.

First Published in 2021 by John Toomey

3rd Edition – July 2025

All inquiries should be made to the author.

A catalogue entry for this book is available from the National Library of Australia.

Printed by Printall Melbourne.
Cover Design by Designware, India (Fiverr)

The paper this book is printed on is certified as environmentally friendly.

Disclaimer

In it for the Long Haul

Making the most of working remotely in the Resources Sector.

3rd Edition

By John Toomey

A Note to the Reader: In Australia there is a term FIFO, which refers to work where the worker Flies In, and Flies Out, living for a period of days or weeks in a remote camp. They may do shifts like 13 and 8, where they work 13 days and then go home for 8 days.

In other countries this term is not used, so for the purposes of this book release in North America, I am adding in the term "Remote Work"

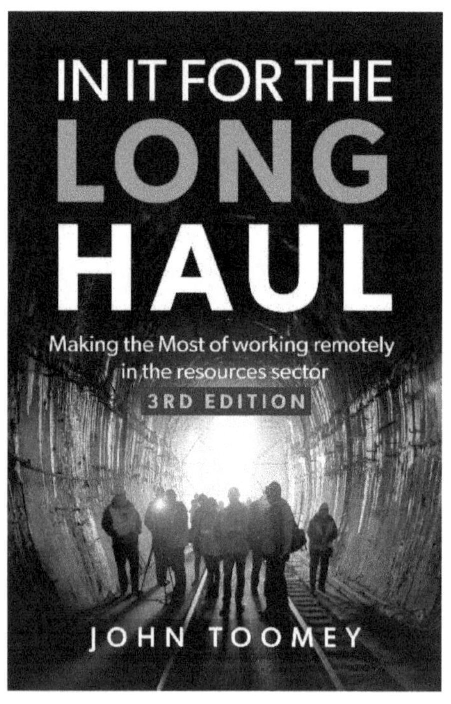

Endorsements

I first met John Toomey in 1998 when he arrived at Richmond to become part of the Coaching Staff. We knew back then he was a bit of a different unit, thinking differently and helping us in ways that many don't consider.

Two years ago, hitting my mid 40's, I became dismayed at how many of my old friends had let themselves go and were now struggling with poor physical and mental health. I wanted to do something about it, so John is the person I turned to. He knows his craft but shares his message with care and humor.

When he shared his book with me, I knew he was on a mission, to care for Australians who are battling and to bring some stability to families and a bright future to the kids they are raising.

Read this book. Not only will it help you, but it will also empower you to help others. You will be supporting John, and myself, to make life better in Australia.

Matthew Richardson
Richmond Football Club
282 games, 800 goals 1993-2009
AFL Hall of Fame, Richmond FC hall of fame
Channel 7 and 3AW AFL broadcast teams 2020 - present

✈ ✈ ✈ ✈ ✈ ✈ ✈ ✈

After a family member moved to Australia recently, I decided to learn as much as I could about the country's history and its unique development. In that process I came across a book called "IN IT FOR THE LONG HAUL"

A good read that examines making the most of the FIFO lifestyle. Having always defined that as first in first out, I was surprised by the Australian meaning of Fly in-Fly out.

It's interesting read that offers a unique perspective on the country's westward expansion and development especially as compared with the US western expansion. The author does a nice job of analyzing the stresses the FIFO lifestyle puts on workers and families.

Finally, the book also offers some tips and observations on personal development that proved both timely and helpful given the stresses of modern-day life.

Charles "Bill" Schneider
Retired former Chairman and CEO of Heath Resources Northwest located in the US Pacific Northwest. Previously Business agent for Graphic International Union

JT is an extraordinary man with deep compassion, empathy and understanding of his fellow humans. His ability to listen and to immerse himself in your story is a rare skill only matched by his desire to improve those around him.

I am so glad he has finally committed some of what is in that wondrous mind to paper. I would like to think it is another gift from him to those of us who know there is still so much room for self-improvement and development.

There are very few like JT, he genuinely cares. This is a must read.

Paul Salmon – AFL Hall of Fame member and Founder/CEO of moodflo.

I first met John in 1982 when he and his colleagues conducted a presentation on training to our state sporting association. At the completion of the evening John offered to all attendees their coaching assistance if required. I took up their offer and never looked back.

John was always a 'trend setter'. Through John's knowledge of strength & conditioning, as well as nutritional programming I was able to improve my performances and win a World Championship in my chosen sport of Para Powerlifting in 1985.

John planted that winning seed of success, and I went on the win 2 more world championships (1991 & 1994) and a gold medal, with a World Record at the 1992 Barcelona Paralympics. He changed my mindset leading into competition which I applied until my retirement in 2000, and still use today.

This is an excellent book for those wishing to take charge of their life, in and out of work. It has practical suggestions and learning exercises to incorporate and assist in making better choices in life.

John is an outstanding person that we are so much better for having as part of our community, a man who has made a difference and who I am so fortunate to have met and even more fortunate to call a friend.

Brian McNicholl
Olympic Gold Medallist, 3 Times World Champion, Word Record Holder

I have known John for over 30 years, and through our shared interests have spent countless hours talking about health and wellbeing. He is a great academic but more importantly is able to take his knowledge and deliver simple concepts.

The life experience and the practical messages allows people to feel comfortable and confident that they can embrace a healthy wonderful meaningful life.

It's a conversation we all must engage in - how can I be better tomorrow than I am today.

Enjoy the journey of the book and learn from a wise authentic human being.

Paul Roos
Founder & Director at Performance by Design
Australian Football Hall of Fame
7 Times All Australian, Twice All Australian Captain 1991-2
All Australian Coach 2005, Leigh Matthews Trophy 1986

AFL Premiership Coach 2005

Foreword

In this life we all have challenges to overcome. Sometimes we make good decisions and other times we don't, but it is always up to us to keep things moving forward in a helpful direction.

The FIFO workforce, many could argue, is a big part of the backbone of the country. Natural Resources create a significant portion of Australia's wealth. For many years, good people have traveled away from home to work in remote regions, often in challenging situations, to serve the needs of our mining corporations, oil and gas companies and a variety of other smaller industries.

Along the way, many pressures have come to play on individuals and families. Marriage breakdowns, addictions, mental illness, and suicide have become common stories.

Yet many would look at the situation from the outside and see the earning potential, the leave breaks between shifts and the lifestyle flexibilities as tickets to prosperity and freedom.

As an Australian and as a father, these things distress me. I wish to see all people living good lives, finding success and happiness, and enjoying the fruits of their labors. But many are not.

I first met John Toomey in the late 90's when he sent me an audio program he created about the relationship between modern nutrition, degenerative disease and environmental breakdown. I knew then that John is a man who cares deeply, and who researches his topics well to come up with solutions that all people can embrace.

In recent times, we have reconnected and still John is a wonderful source of wise guidance and clear thinking. It seems his foundational mission is to improve life, for others.

So, when John shared that he was writing this book, and that he hoped I would write a foreword, I could not accept fast enough.

In these pages, you will find sound guidance, useable strategies, and thought-provoking perspectives, all written with a deep level of care. I feel that John's wish is for you and your family is that the FIFO lifestyle will bring you stability, success, and fulfillment.

Enjoy

Greg Chappell AO, MBE – Former Australian Cricket Captain

Introduction

What an opportunity! Imagine getting to travel to some of the most naturally beautiful parts of the world to work, to live an existence where you work two weeks on and one week off (or a similar variation of shift), earning good money.

The food is ok, the accommodation adequate and the work is interesting. There is not much to spend your money on, so saving is easy. And when you get home for your time off, there are no work-life worries to bring with you. It seems to be a good deal.

So why do so many suffer from depression, anxiety, and loneliness? Why are so many taking their own lives? Why are so many relationships falling apart? So many are watching it happen, and many are worrying about it, but why is it occurring? How can we change it?

This book aims to explore and reveal how you can turn FIFO into an extraordinary experience. Along the journey, we will explore the lifestyle, the potential causes of mental illness, the many opportunities for outstanding achievement and happiness, and eventually present a formula for making it work. I wish that everyone who engages in FIFO work, whether for a few years or an entire career, gets to make the most of it and make it a most loved part of their life.

From Viktor Frankl: *"Everything can be taken from a man but one thing: the last of the human freedoms—to choose one's attitude in any given set of circumstances, to choose one's own way."*

My personal experience of FIFO is limited, and it was a long time ago. So, I wanted to make that clear, upfront. However, I have travelled with work for years and consistently stayed away for about 240 nights per year for many years.

In recent years, however, since 2007, I have travelled as a speaker and as a teacher of a Self-development Course. These courses required me to live in the venue where the program was delivered for 11 or 12 days, twelve to fifteen times per year, and worked 13 to 15 hours per day.

These courses were conducted in Australia, New Zealand, and the USA. Some years I travelled to the US seven or eight times.

I also did part of my growing up in a pub in a small town called Miles in Queensland in the 1960s. Most of our regular lodgers were people travelling for work, many of those construction workers building Wheat Silos for Transfield. I spent many hours as a young kid, sitting and talking to these wonderfully kind men who worked hard during the day and took solace in the peaceful evenings, chatting to myself and my siblings while they missed their families.

And I remember well my Mum's story. She was born and raised on a Cattle Station between Roma and Surat in Queensland. She told us of the cattle hands and drovers who roamed the country looking for work, often to support their families left behind in another part of Australia. I, too, was born there and lived on the station till I was four. So, I have clear memories of many of those men, sleeping on bunk beds in the stockman's quarters and telling stories over enamel mugs of hot tea.

Mum studied in Roma to be a nurse when she finished school. Once she was qualified, Mum was posted to Mareeba in Far North Queensland. This was not a "13 days on, six days off" scenario. It was over 18 months after starting work that she got to see her family again.

When I was 18, I secured a job with Nationwide Catering, serving as a kitchen hand on the Bass Straight Gas Platforms. I worked, from memory, about eight days on and then six days off. The money was excellent. I was amazed that we had to prepare four different entrees, main courses, and desserts for every meal, and enough of each if all the workers wanted just one of the options. Over-eating was normal.

Twenty years later, I was back there delivering Men's Health Seminars to an obese workforce. While the extreme menu requirements were a union demand back in the '70s, the company feared a lawsuit from a diseased team member.

As far as I can tell, whilst FIFO as we know it may be a relatively new phenomenon to many, people have been travelling hundreds and sometimes thousands of kilometres to create an opportunity to earn money to support their families for many decades.

Suppose we stop for a moment and look at the number of roads, railway lines, bridges, and telegraph poles all over regional Australia. In that case, we realise that someone left home for indefinite periods to do back-breaking work, sleeping in tents by the road, eating camp food and battling the elements. Can you even begin to imagine the hardship in those roles as 19th and 20th-century pioneers forged an infrastructure into this wild and brutal country?

Every April 25th, we celebrate the spirit of the ANZACS. But, I often think we should also celebrate the same spirit in the hardy beings who built this country; men and women who left their homes and headed off toward the horizon in service to a growing nation or simply to earn a quid.

I am also amazed at the number of women and men from The Philippines and Indonesia who leave their home country and travel abroad to work to send money back to their families. Grandparents are often left to raise the children as Mum and Dad head out into the world to make a lonely living. Women work as live-in housekeepers, maids, and child-carers for wealthy families in China, Japan, and Korea. The men travel to serve as construction workers right across Asia and The Middle East.

Often the safety standards on these construction jobs are well below what we would accept in Australia, and these people are often viewed as second class citizens. They are subjected to harsh and often demeaning treatment at the hands of their employers.

So, as we start this journey, I would like to celebrate the Australian based companies that employ FIFO workforces. First, I acknowledge the enormous risks they take and the profound investments made to get a project to the starting line. Locating profitable mineral deposits or oil reservoirs is no easy task.

In this system, companies transport workers to and from the site in great comfort; they provide comfortable and private accommodation, plenty of freshly prepared food, recreational facilities, internet access, excellent pay, perhaps the safest working conditions globally, governed by fair and equitable laws. As an old friend of mine used to say, "It's a pretty good gig!"

On the other hand, indeed, they often cannot guarantee long-term job security. Markets fluctuate, mineral deposits and oil reserves diminish, economies often slow down, and demand often changes. Moreover, some projects have a definite length, like construction jobs, while others are subject to unpredictable factors.

All of this means that working FIFO can be unpredictable and lacking in security. It can mean months off work with no pay, losing money on real estate investments, and being forced to relocate to different parts of the country. It can be a rocky ride.

My aim in writing this book is to explore the "nitty-gritty" of FIFO while keeping an eye on a much bigger picture. I seek to help you prepare for the work to optimise your experience, whether you are going solo, or leaving your family, or if you are the partner or family member left at home.

This book is about bringing understanding, peace of mind and comfort to you whilst supporting you to achieve your goals and create a great life.

"Life is what happens when you are busy making other plans." – **John Lennon**

"There are a lot of things I wish I would have done, instead of just sitting around and complaining about having a boring life." – **Kurt Cobain**

"Should be compulsory reading for everybody in Australia, in the world…and even beyond. And you can quote me on that."
- Elliot Goblet Comedian and Funny MC.

Table of Contents

"Where you are now is where you once decided you wanted to be. There is no sense in second guessing the wisdom behind the decision. It made sense at the time."

Harry Palmer

This is Life

Before I get into the core of this book and begin discussing the issues, I would like to explore some things with you and, I would like to start by revealing some of my own beliefs.

Life is, in many ways, just one big mystery. Who knows what it is all about? Is there a purpose to it? Nobody knows for sure. Many have theories, and many choose to believe certain things. Perhaps that is what gives their life meaning.

I promise I am not about to go all religious on you. I did grow up a Roman Catholic and went to some great Catholic schools, but by the time I was 21, too much of it was not sitting well with me, so I walked out of Mass early one Sunday and never went back.

But I did have many questions, eating away in the depths of my being, wondering what it was all about. Perhaps that was stimulated by my religious education as it probably raised my curiosity and gave me more questions than it did answers.

That left me with this unyielding curiosity about life. I have rarely ever had a job where I have worked for someone else. I have always owned businesses, often contracting myself to organisations like AFL Clubs, but somehow, I had to keep mapping my own course. There was never holiday pay from an employer or other related benefits, but it has been a rich experience.

I kept reading books and met fascinating people. Some became my teachers and mentors, and others played their part in providing me with life lessons: some harsh, some amazing.

I remember turning a corner when I read "The Road Less Travelled" by M. Scot Peck. If you like to read, I certainly recommend it. It is certainly not the end game, but it is a wonderful start.

I guess the thing I got from that book, the "brutal truth" I found, was – It is not all about me!

It was most liberating. I re-awoke to the incredible power of contributing to others, to finding ways in life to be helpful, to give attention to supporting the welfare of others and contributing when and where I could. I realised that my selfishness was suffocating me and taking away my creativity, my joy, and my inspiration for living.

As I travelled more, read more books, and met many more people, I became vitally interested in the value of community. Very few people can do it on their own, in some form of isolation. Even Monks who spend many hours a day in silent meditation still live in a community.

I have known of the occasional person who decides to step away from the community and live an isolated and solitary existence, but those people are most rare.

We live in communities. Those communities can be our family, neighbourhood, workplace, local footy club, college, church, or even a movement we might be connected to like a service organisation, a hobby group, or even a political party.

The real magic of life presents itself when we discover the joy in the contribution we can make to that community instead of calculating what that community might give to us. And contributions may be big or small. That does not matter. The rewards come because, when you give selflessly, you find a fantastic feeling of satisfaction. You start liking who you are.

During my time working in high-performance roles in AFL clubs, I developed a close relationship with a young guy who was an exceptional talent. He went on to become one of the best players of his era. His athleticism was rare, and he could kick a footy out of sight.

He started out playing senior football in his first season as an 18-year-old. After a few games, he was dropped to the seconds to learn some lessons to help him be better prepared for the pressure of the 1st 18.

Playing at Centre Half Back, he dominated every week, got 30 possessions, and took many marks. But each week he was selected in the reserves. He became bewildered as to what he had to do to gain senior selection.

I asked the senior coach what he had to do, and he replied, "He is getting heaps of the footy, but so is his man. His opponents always hurt us. So, he must learn to stop his opponent."

I asked the coach if that had been made clear to the kid, and he assured me it had. So, it seemed the message was not getting through.

The next day I took the young fellow out to a café to have a coffee, and I said to him. "Imagine you live in a tribal village, and you are the chief. Everyone has their grass hut, and many animals are walking around like dogs, goats, sheep, cows and pigs, plus chickens and geese. One of the challenges in the village is that the animals shit everywhere, including outside your front door, and a daily chore for everyone is shovelling up the shit. So your problem, mate, is that you are enjoying all the trappings of being the chief, but you are not shovelling your share of the shit!"

His eyes nearly popped out. I then continued, "When you pick up your man and stop him getting the ball, you are taking care of your teammates. You are shovelling your share of the shit!"

It landed for him. That week, he was best afield, and his opponent hardly touched the footy. The following week he was back in the 1st 18 and never looked back. He played in a Premiership team.

We have all noticed how a young child responds when they have done something nice for their Mum or Dad. How they feel about themselves at that moment is palpable. So it is in our DNA to be giving and caring.

So, let us take a more expansive look at this life.

"There's nowhere you can be that isn't where you're meant to be..." – John Lennon

This Incredible Thing Called Life

Sometimes it is easy to lose our perspective on life. We can get caught up in our perceptions and impressions of what is going on around us and lose our way. Taking a step back and contemplating where 'you are at and where you are headed is often helpful to enable you to refocus and gain clarity.

What Would You Do?

If I were to give you a Gold Pass today, and you could use it to enter the life you want tomorrow, and that life would be accompanied by the pay packet you seek, what would you do?

What would you do? What would your life look like?

Perhaps you are not sure? Maybe this is a question you have not contemplated in years. But it is a question worth serious consideration. In short, are you living the life that you choose to live, or are you living the life that you feel you should be living?

Maybe you are driven by things like:

- Financial needs
- Obligations
- Other People's Expectations
- Social Norms
- Your Indoctrinated view of how you should be
- Fear of failure

Putting all of that aside, what would you love to do in your life? What is that thing that is deep In your heart that would make your life so full of passion and excitement that you would never have time for worry, anxiety, or boredom?

Another Question

One day you will die, and you will be cremated or buried. That is pretty much a fact unless you believe something else. On that day, someone, perhaps one of your adult children, is going to stand up and deliver a eulogy.

What will they say? What is that thing that you did in your life that they are going to talk about? What was the primary, most significant impression that you will have left?

What piece of wisdom would you like to share with your favourite grandchild on your death bed? Would it be something like, "Wow, kid! What a life. I never missed out on having a crack at anything I wanted to do. And look what I created. Look at how my life has helped other people."

Or will I be something like, "Well, at least I never missed an episode of CSI!"

It is hard to live an inspired life if you are not doing what you love and deeply passionate about.

It Does not have to be your Career.

Maybe your passion is not something you can do for a living. Perhaps you have a passion for coaching and teaching kids in your favourite sport. Perhaps you love soccer, and you want to coach kids, help them explore the game, and maximise their sport experience.

Now you might not be able to find a paid position. Your daytime job might be something you do to make money so that you may live your passion.

Once I was running some Life Balance seminars at a company. The company employed a man, an Iraqi immigrant, who was not a happy camper and challenging to deal with. So I asked the manager to find out what this man's passion was.

It turned out that the man was deeply passionate about Football; he was completely disconnected from it. In his home country, he had been a talented player. A few inquiries later turned up a junior team in the man's local area struggling to find a coach. The man was introduced to the club and set about building a team, passionately sharing his knowledge with some very appreciative young kids. It was not long before the whole workplace was taking an interest in the team.

The man became happy and settled into the workplace, and became popular among his workmates.

Where do your passions lie? Have you discovered your true purpose?

Your Lighthouse

Imagine you get tipped out of your boat, 3km off the beach in the evening. A storm has kicked up, and you are treading water in rough seas. It is all you can do to simply keep your head above water and avoid being swamped by waves.

You can tread water and hope that you will survive till daylight and that someone will come and find you. But then, as you panic and struggle, off in the distance, you see a lighthouse.

You now have a choice. You can remain where you are and continue to struggle to keep your head above water. Or you can begin moving toward the lighthouse.

Only one choice will give you a chance of survival.

In life, we all need a lighthouse to move toward. When we discover that passion, that thing that excites us deep to the core, then we can begin moving toward it.

Where is your lighthouse? If life is a struggle, what are you going to stretch toward? Consider this analogy of a minute.

Put it down on Paper.

To help you out, start to make notes about your passion as you explore the possibilities. This may take 10 minutes. It may take ten weeks. The time does not matter if you are moving closer to getting a clear handle on what you are here to do.

Once you get it down and clear, write down a concise description of where you are right now.

Finally, look at the two options and ask yourself, "What is it that is standing between where you are now and where you want to be?" It is probably your life as you have created it to this time.

How do you change it? The first step is to gain more of an understanding of life.

Who is in Control of Your Life?

For too long, we have been in automatic pilot. Waking in time to get to work, often eating breakfast on the run and arriving at work in a rushed state. We work all day, drink too much coffee and tea, fail to eat enough nutritious food, and head for home again, often after dark.

At home, we face the television, a tired and often stressed family or partner, quite often too much food and a late night.

That is not how it is meant to be. We should be waking refreshed, getting some exercise, and eating a nutritious breakfast. Then, leaving for work at a reasonable time, arriving relaxed and working efficiently, with energy, throughout the day. We should leave at an appropriate time to come home reasonably fresh and relaxed at the day's end. We can then prepare a nutritious meal, spend time with the family or friends and retire at a reasonable time to ensure a restful sleep.

What has happened to us? We have lost control, and we are not taking responsibility for that loss of control. We have forgotten what real life and actual survival is. Instead, we have become all-consuming hedonists, worried only about what we think is owed to us and what we deserve to receive.

Would You Survive?

If I were to take you out into the middle of the Simpson Desert and leave you, all alone, would you be able to make it back to civilisation, to water and to the things that will ensure your survival?

This question invites you to think about yourself and your personal resources. Have you still got that "hard edge" humans need to survive in tough times? Or have you become so domesticated and soft that losing simple luxuries like television can be enough to ruin your life?

When we look around at the levels of obesity, ill health, and over-indulgence, we see a population of people who do not have a basic fitness level that would allow them to run for a bus. So, where are we headed as a nation and as individuals?

The cold hard facts of the matter tell us that people are no longer hardened to the task of fighting for their survival. People's physical survival is not challenged every day, so they are not trained to deal with a situation where their survival is compromised. The skills required to survive include:

- The fitness and strength to walk for many hours, perhaps for days.
- The capacity to endure thirst and hunger and the strength to self-ration food and water supplies.
- The capacity to calculate direction, recognise and monitor landmarks and stay on a path toward a destination.
- To find food and water in the wilderness.
- To overcome the fear and loneliness associated with the isolation of being separated from civilisation.
- The capacity to remain positive and to keep working toward solving the problem.

The Necessity of Struggle

It is the fight for survival that keeps us lean, hungry and able. Imagine living a life where you had to work hard physically to get food each day, where shelter was something that required physical work daily and, your safety was not guaranteed simply due to exposure to the elements and the presence of possible assailants.

When we do not have to fight or struggle for our survival, we lose that hard edge. When we lose that edge, we become soft and weak. Minor hindrances become big hindrances. Small problems become big problems. We lose perspective. We forget what it took to win our peace, security, and tranquillity.

In our lives, as we face each challenge, we have a choice: Go through or avoid. When we go through, we learn, we gain strength wisdom.

When we avoid, nothing happens other than a lowering of our self-respect. I do not doubt that those challenges we avoid will continue to revisit us, dressed in a different costume, until we learn the lesson we need to learn. Then we can move on.

Warriors face their challenges and push through to the other side. Victims run and hide. Which are you? A Warrior? Or a Victim?

A Look at History

If we look back over our knowledge of history, we realise that many societies have been to this place before. For example, the Romans, Greeks, Egyptians, Persians, Aztecs, and Incas all reached a point where they dominated their environment and lived in a state of profound abundance.

Studies of the Roman Empire showed that they were a hardened, warrior type nation that deliberately expanded its borders. They took over lands and societies as they went, either by negotiation or by force and as their technological advancements followed, the empire produced, and economies developed. And the wealth flowed back to Rome.

Over this time, as some benefitted and others did not, and as the expansion of the empire slowed, people became disenfranchised and unhappy with their lot. Diverting the peoples' attention away from the inequities of life, the ruling class staged the games in the Colosseums, where soldiers marched in to re-enact the great battles of the past. The hapless Gladiators faced almost certain death at the hands of the nation's heroes.

What happens to a society when people become so intensely captivated and entertained by something so mindless and grotesque? But when we look around today and see our community consumed with people on television throwing tantrums and misbehaving as they compete in apartment block renovation shows or cooking competitions, are we not succumbing to the same.

Reality Television tells us that Australian Society is bored and uninspired. We succumb to the temptations of base-level behaviours of others to find our entertainment and perhaps to feel better about ourselves.

To find happiness, we need to reach for something much better and hold ourselves to higher ideals and higher standards.

Fight or Flight and the Ego

Fight or Flight is the body's natural response to danger. Imagine you were born and raised in Africa, and one day, whilst walking through the forest, you see a sizeable carnivorous cat stalking you. At that moment, every signalling system in your body switches on to survival. Within the blink of an eye, your adrenal glands are secreting adrenalin at a frantic rate. Your heart rises, ready to deliver blood to your muscles. Your respiration rate increases to deliver oxygen to the bloodstream, the arteries in the top half of your body constrict, and the arteries in the lower half dilate, ready to provide blood to the muscles of the legs and hips. Finally, your bowels open to dump any extra load. Hence the term "shit yourself". You are now ready to "Run for your life."

What happens next? Well, you will either be eaten, which means you have nothing left to worry about. Or you make your escape. And when you do, you will have run so hard, all the adrenaline will have been burned off, and there will be no residual feelings of stress or worry.

This is a Survival response. Fight or Flight. Do I stay and fight for my life, or do I run? Either way, your adrenal glands have you well prepared. But it is meant to be a short-term thing.

But here comes the sticky part. We create the same response when the survival of our ego is under threat. If we have been dishonest and are about to be found out, guess what? Fight or Flight response. But it is worse because there is no intense bout of exercise, and the threat is gone. The danger may remain for some time; sad stuff. A prolonged period of high adrenalin response leaves you feeling exhausted and sets you up for sickness.

As soon as our ego gets a little carried away with itself, it may become vulnerable to some form of attack, compromise, humiliation, or exposure.

One of the best ways to avoid this type of stress is to live a humble life. But often, cashed up FIFO workers get a little carried away, and their ego goes out of control. The pending humiliation in a downturn can be catastrophic and often leads to terrible outcomes. More on that later.

Cast Away

Like many great films, the theme behind Cast Away is a powerful message designed to teach us something. Here was a man, the ultimate ego, with no regard for the critically essential things in life like love, family, community, and personal wellbeing.

Defined by his title, his pager and his watch, Hank's character was loud, obnoxious and "Federal Express" to the core. When he landed on the island, he had no food or water and no resources to help him get both. He did have some FedEx parcels, but he was not going to open those. No matter how desperate his situation was, he could not abandon his identity. His identity defined him.

As desperation grew, he looked at the alter he had subconsciously built (FedEx parcels with watch and pager on top) and realised that perhaps his survival might depend on what was inside those parcels. So began the process of "tearing back the layers". This moment is symbolic of a person tearing away the layers of themselves to find out who they really are.

As he tore through the layers, he came across "Wilson", the soccer ball. With his bloody handprint, Hanks' character inadvertently makes a face on the ball. As he sits it up on a pile of boxes, it stares at him. The fight between the ego (Hanks) and his true self (symbolised by the ball) begins in earnest, with the ego kicking and screaming to maintain its failing status. As time passes, the ego quiets, and the character assumes the role of survivor, and quiet contemplation follows. The final transition occurs when he is forced to knock out his aching tooth.

In the end, he has assumed his own true identity. His is a hero's journey, and he is returning home. He loses Wilson because he no longer needs him. Thus, he returns, a man of wisdom and integrity, someone who has a new and profound appreciation of life.

In this modern life, perhaps our egos have taken over. Competitiveness and striving to accumulate possessions, our ideas of what success is, encourage us to build an impression that we are successful. This behaviour is ego-building, and we begin to live through it. But the ego often struggles with entitlement and self-importance, tends to have little integrity or moral values, and seeks self-interest over the best interests of others. I have been there many times. I suspect we all have.

It is essential for each of us to be aware of our egos, explore them, explore ourselves, discover our true nature, and discover who we really are.

Even the name of the movie tells us. It is not "Castaway" but "Cast Away" – meaning to cast away an "out of control" and life-limiting ego.

What is Life all about?

For centuries, people have used their religion as a strong guiding force in their lives. However, since the 1960s, people have been abandoning religion in droves, seeking to break out from what was perceived to be patriarchal dominance and a lack of personal freedom and expression of free will.

Religious practice gave people a "code" of behaviour. Many religions used liberal doses of fear to motivate their followers to 'remain on the straight and narrow path'. But a study of the pure essences of the teachings of the great masters like Buddha, Jesus Christ, Mohammed, Krishna, and others reveals something much more profound and yet something quite simple.

Life is a journey - a quest for discovery. It is a journey of learning about the self and seeking to live out one's potential and maximise the learning this life provides. Along the path, we face a variety of challenges, some small and others quite large. These challenges are perhaps designed to provide us with the impetus for growth as people. Without growth, we wither and die.

Indeed, with challenges and hardship, we learn about ourselves. We learn our strengths and weaknesses, and we begin to understand our capacity to endure. It is interesting to note that we all start at school at the age of five or six on what appears to be a level playing field. We all do the same educational lessons daily for years. Yet some of us turn out to be doctors and others concreters. Some become amazing athletes and others talented artists. Some have many difficulties in relationships, while others find a soul mate for life and become loving parents. We all respond to life's challenges differently. We all learn different lessons, and we all progress at different rates with varying degrees of resistance or enthusiasm.

As these challenges face us, the ego will often scream and shout about how unfair it all is. It may take on a victim mentality. However, our "true self" will see the challenge for what it is, realise the importance of standing up to the challenge and be prepared to endure whatever pain and suffering the challenge holds.

Many of these challenges are most difficult. Consider some of them.

- Starting a Training Program when you are unfit
- Leaving a bad relationship
- Starting a new job
- Moving to a new city
- The loss of a loved one
- Financial failure
- Illness or injury and many others
- Working out how to find joy in working FIFO

With a difficult challenge comes a degree of pain and suffering. But pain is nothing more than fertiliser. It is fuel for growth. When you are feeling pain, you are growing. These challenges provide the impetus for growth as people. Without growth, we wither and die.

Love versus Fear

Human beings are born out of love. Apart from a minimal number of seemingly accidental births, human life is created from an act of love. A baby engenders a strong feeling of love in all of us. When we were born, each of us was an example of pure love.

Some of us have been lucky enough to have extremely wise, patient, and caring parents and grandparents to nurture us and never allow us to lose this sense of love.

For many, however, fear crept into the equation and never really left. Consider a small child becoming lost in a large crowd, perhaps in a shopping mall. The child is stricken with terror, experiencing fear for the first time, and eventually experiencing emotional hurt.

The events that follow this experience are critical. The child will feel insecure and will not want to experience a re-occurrence of the hurt. Next time the parent declares that another trip to the mall is about to occur, the fear may return, resulting in perhaps a tantrum or some other sort of "bad behaviour". If the parent is aware of the reason for the behaviour, reassurance, and a promise that the child will be carried, the entire time may relieve the anxiety.

However, if the parent, rushed and stressed, decides to "put the behaviour down", they simply force the child into a state of anxiety. At this point, the child feels anger and resentment. Unable to communicate this clearly to the parent, the child begins to behave in rebellious and somewhat objectionable ways.

Again, the aware parent will move to correct the problem through understanding and reassurance. The unaware parent may then become angry at the child. When the parent becomes angry, the child then becomes confused and then may perhaps begin to think that they are, in fact, the problem. When this occurs, the child starts to recognise the behaviours they demonstrate that bring a positive response from the parents. For example, the child learns to "tap dance" to get a positive reaction from the parent.

Soon, the child builds a "personality" that is acceptable. It is essential to understand the needs of a human being. Simply, we need:

- Clean Air
- Fresh Water
- Nutritious Food
- Shelter (including clothing)
- Love (which means to be able to give and receive love and to be included in a community)
- Purpose (to feel that one is making a valid contribution to that community)

These needs are the foundations upon which our life is built. If you imagine your persona as a house, these are the stumps.

When we take this almost typical journey through our growing years, we often build a different persona than the one we started out with. The impressions created by emotional hurt have forced us to construct a façade that tells the world we are okay, that it is alright to like us, love us, and include us in the community. This façade is created from fear.

LOVE: We are born out of Love. An infant is perhaps the purest example of Love. As a baby, we are completely loved, and our Love for our parents and those we recognise receive our unfettered Love.

HURT: At some point, we experience Hurt. Maybe as a toddler, we get lost in a shopping mall. It can be a terrifying experience, but once we are reunited with our loved ones, we are ok. But we have experienced hurt.

ANGER: Then perhaps comes anger. Maybe next time Mum and Dad want to go to the mall, we are not too keen on the idea. We resist. If mum and dad are understanding, perhaps they can broker a deal that we accept. But maybe they are just in a hurry, and they force our hand. Now we are angry at being forced.

But as we go, our anger attracts disapproval.

SHAME: Our anger is rejected. We start to find other ways to let our anger out, and that draws an angry response. Soon, we find that we are losing connection with those we love. That vital need for a community is drifting. Perhaps then we begin to doubt ourselves and how we are creating our life. We begin to feel shame and guilt.

PRETENSE and EGO: So, we set about building a persona that will ensure our connection to our community. It creates behaviours that will attract favour and approval. But, the new persona promises much more than it can deliver. It is a lie being used to attract love.

IT CAN ALL BE DEVELOPED ON FEAR: This development of the ego perhaps starts when we first felt fear and it was not handled well. In many cases, this type of Ego is built on old fears.

The Ego can be a facade that hides what we need to grow through.

Your Life as a House

Imagine your life as a quaint little house with everything to give you a good life. It is warm, solid, enduring, warm, secure and inviting. The stumps that create the foundation for this house are the basic needs I talked of earlier, Air, Water, Food, Shelter, Community and Purpose.

When we get to the "shame" part of the path (outlined above), we start to look at our house as deficient somehow. We begin to think that it is insignificant and will not be noticed in this street and nobody will bother to visit.

So, we decide that we cannot change the house, but we can create a new facade to make it look more impressive. But this facade is large, heavy, and often unstable, and it needs more stumps to support it. So, then we go looking for stumps, needs that will sustain the ego we are creating.

These needs can take all sorts of forms. Some may include:

- The latest mobile phone
- A new outfit every week
- A house that we cannot afford in an "impressive suburb"
- Perhaps it is a car or similar asset that we cannot afford
- For some, it is a new relationship with a younger partner when we hit our middle age

When these things are challenged or perhaps taken away, we can react with a similar stress response to the one we might feel when we lose love or cannot get enough air. This situation can be the source of a great deal of modern stress.

Do you doubt your "house"? Are you building a facade that is way too difficult to maintain?

Once we arrive at the point in our lives where the ego is fully developed, we struggle through, trying to maintain this facade, worrying about what other people think, trying to impress.

The Way Home

Eventually, we must turn and start, through our challenges, to break down the false façade we have built to find our true self that was born into the world so many years ago.

Wouldn't you like to discover who you really are? You are not what your teachers, or mates or even your family labelled you as. That is just a version of you that they believe they know. But in your own quiet time, you know you are more than that.

Things can get sticky when you start believing the labels you have allowed others to place on you, especially the negative labels. It can take a bit of work to unstick yourself from those.

There are generally two fundamental human motivational forces. All emotional responses tend to arise from these. They are love and fear. Ask yourself. Are you motivated by Love or Fear?

Fear is the emotion that makes us tap dance. It makes us seek approval, and it makes us keep on placing ourselves in positions of high stress simply to feel loved or accepted, to feel secure. It is the emotion that has us assert that we are something other than who we are, impressive, or imposing or important. It is a bazaar twist.

A relationship cannot be healthy if one partner lives in fear of losing the other. Soon, their insecurity will destroy the relationship. For example, a team leader cannot survive if their team is in fear of them. If they are fearful, they will not speak their mind. Hence, the leader will never have their views challenged and will not grow as a leader.

The true self acts out of love. Love comes in many forms, from romantic love to nurturing love to tough love. Sometimes, we need a bit more tough love to stop the ego from taking over with its victim mentality.

The ego often acts out of fear. It avoids being challenged and will usually make its judgements based on the fear of being challenged. I could advise you not to act out of fear, but it is not easy when it is running on automatic.

As challenges confront us, the ego may scream and shout about how unfair it all is. It may well take on a victim mentality. However, the true self, that person who we really are underneath all our pretence, will see the challenge for what it is, realise the importance of standing up to the challenge and be prepared to endure whatever pain and suffering the challenge holds.

Are you a victim? Are you blaming others for making your life difficult? Where you are in your life now is a product of your decisions on the way to arriving here. You are here as a result of your actions and decisions thus far.

Sure, you may have had a super tricky start or some major tragedies along the way, but even then, you made decisions. There is much to learn if you look with interest at your life thus far. You will know where you made bad decisions or when you did things you are not proud of.

So, what do you do? Do you continue to play victim, or do you get on with the business of living?

Note: *There are many other ways to look at ego and many ways to explore ego. I doubt we would have a Sydney Harbour Bridge or an MCG if it were not for someone's ego. The Ego can become a bit of a challenge when it starts to get a little drunk on its own fumes. Some humility is needed, or perhaps humiliation may follow. It is good to read about ego and identity and explore the topic with interest and curiosity.*

You have a choice

So, Warrior or Victim. Are you going to learn your life lessons, or will you be a victim and blame others for your misery? It is up to you. On the other hand, you can be a modern warrior, forging a path through life, taking your challenges like a mature adult and setting an example for the people around you.

Or, you can just go and have another beer, fold your arms and wait for someone else to take the lead.

The Challenge

So, are you being challenged enough in your life? Are you growing at a rate conducive to happiness and self-satisfaction? Are you on the way to becoming the person you want to be?

An old mentor of mine used to say, "When you are green you grow, and when you are ripe you rot!" Keeping yourself in a situation where you are not quite sure what to do keeps an element of struggle in your life, forcing you to grow and adapt.

So, where are your challenges? If you do not feel you have adequate challenges right now, then perhaps you should go and find one before one that you might not like comes looking for you.

The areas that you need to keep challenging so that you remain strong and vibrant in those areas are:

- Work
- Relationship
- Parenting
- Friendships
- Community
- Fitness and Health
- Emotions
- Spiritual Growth and Awareness
- Mental and Intellectual Development
- Personal Adventure

Throwing all your energy into just one or two of these areas is foolhardy and limiting. You know that if your relationship goes off the rails, your work performance will plummet. However, I suggest that putting a lot of attention on expanding your awareness will have a significant pay-off in all other areas. So, what is your next challenge?

Your Working Life

Your working life can be the place that gives you your most significant challenges. The tasks, the people and the situations can teach you a great deal about yourself. So what sort of contribution are you making in your workplace?

Taking on a FIFO Role may well be one of the best challenges you have ever explored. So many areas of your life are being stretched, including your relationships, personal resilience, time management, ability to avoid temptation and your capacity to work long hours.

Perhaps you might like to take on some additional challenges like pursuing some online study, a new fitness goal, or possibly reading some books. It is your gig. How do you want it to shape you? Let us explore this further in the following sections.

Discipline is a Key!

How often have you heard the term "You have to be more disciplined!" Somewhere in that statement lies a promise that once you are disciplined, then everything will be easy.

A few years back, I was chatting to my old friend and mentor, Tommy Hafey. If you do not know who Tommy was, he coached Richmond to 4 Premierships in the VFL and successfully coached Collingwood, Geelong, and Sydney. He was a good player himself and became one of the most "in demand" speakers in Australia.

Tommy was legendary for his unbreakable fitness routines. Every morning, he got out of bed at 5:30, ran 8 km, then he would strip down to his speedos, do 15 minutes of stretching on the beach, 250 push-ups and then go in for a swim, 365 days per year.

After the swim, he would go home and do 600 sit-ups. Then three or four times per week, he would go to the gym and lift weights.

I would often see Tommy out there in the mornings when I was on my run. We would always say hello and sometimes stop for a bit of a chat. It was always a treat to ask, "How are you, Tommy?" His replies were gold. My favourite, "I am sensational, but there is no need to worry because I am getting better!"

One day, I dropped by his place for a cup of tea and a chat. I asked him what his secret was to get up and go for it every morning. What did he do to make it so easy? His reply:

"Easy. This morning I woke. I had a late night. My first thought was about how tired I was and how I probably needed more sleep. I started agreeing with myself. That went on for about 5 minutes, and I nearly went back to sleep, but this voice deep inside said, 'Get outta bed you lazy bastard', and I got up and went for my run."

He shared that he had never found it easy and that most mornings, he fought with himself to make it happen. I am the same.

All humans love comfort. It is easier to sit on the sofa than it is to stand up and do ten squats. It is easier to stay in bed and snuggle than to get up and make your bed, especially when it is cold.

Discipline has nothing to do with anything being easy. It has everything to do with deciding. When you have goals, things you want to achieve, sometimes you must decide every day, sometimes many times in a single day.

Think for a moment what it would take to give up smoking.

Discipline comes from you committing to a goal. Once your goal is obvious, you know where you are going. Then you will need a plan to get there. Once that is clear, your commitment is to action your plan. Discipline is the quality you need to action that daily plan, even when you do not want to.

Will you slip up? I am sure you will. But a slip up is just a slip up unless you use it as an excuse to give up. You are a human being.

If we happen to be talking about Physical Training here, for example, you choose to follow a fitness program; then one thing is most important. If you miss a day, do not try to squeeze it in. You are creating difficulty that will lead you to miss more days.

A bad day is a bad day. Leave it be. Move on.

The Grass is Brown on Both Sides of the Fence

If you are not enjoying your life, you may ask yourself what or who needs to change. Blaming your circumstance may not be the answer.

For example, you might not like the site you are working on. Will going to another project make things better? Perhaps it will, and perhaps it will not.

Many people I have spoken to, some close to me, move from job to job and find themselves disliking their situation. Eventually, some realise they might find a better outcome if they stop blaming their environment and begin looking at their own attitude.

If you do not like yourself, changing your environment will not fix anything.

"No one is afraid of heights, they're afraid of falling down. No one is afraid of saying I love you, they're afraid of the answer." – Kurt Cobain

Chapter Summary

Where are you at, and where are you headed?

What would you do in this life if everything lined up for you? What would you go for?

When you die, people will tell your story. Perhaps you would like it to sound a certain way.

Your life passion and your career do not have to be the same thing. Sometimes you need a job to earn money whilst you follow your passions.

Take time to explore your lighthouse. Find the passion that will light your life path.

Where are you headed, and where are you now? What stands between where you are now and where you are headed?

Reminding yourself who is in control of your life and your decisions.

If you got stuck out in the middle of nowhere, do you have what it takes to survive and find your way back home? If not, why not? Unfortunately, many of us have lost our resilience.

A look at history tells us what happens to great civilizations when they become wealthy, and life becomes easeful. They perish. Our country is now wealthy, and everything is quite easy.

Many Australians are bored because they have removed all the challenges from their lives. They would rather watch someone else do it on TV, whilst they remain comfortable.

How much is your ego getting in the way? Are you a bit like Chuck Noland from Cast Away? Are you prepared to become humble?

Life is a journey, and our challenges are the fuel we can use to grow, evolve, and improve. So, what challenges can you deliberately take on to force yourself to grow?

Are you a Warrior or a Victim?

Are you seeking attention and approval from others, or are you giving your attention to the areas of life that need it most – to relieve suffering and raise up the less fortunate? What are the personas you are creating in your life? Are they helpful?

Separate your genuine needs from your wants. Confusing wants with needs is one of the things that can create difficulty in your life.

Love versus Fear. Which one will you allow to be the driving motivational force in your life?

You have a choice. You can take this as a challenge right now and decide, if you wish, to start walking the road less traveled and take on a more rewarding life that will help you to grow and evolve.

Your working life can be the key. How you approach your FIFO experience can be everything you need to create rich experiences full of growth and learning.

All you need is a goal that clearly defines the person you want to become, some discipline and a willingness to enjoy the journey.

Life Tips from This Chapter

This is your life. You have as much right to finding your passion as any person you know or about whom you have read. So many give up on finding their passion. Please do not do that to yourself. And if you have not yet discovered it, then keep exploring. When you find it, you will discover true inspiration and peace.

Here are some tips:

- What were you deeply interested in when you were 10, or 13 or 16 or even 18? Write those things down.
- When you open a newspaper, what sort of stories make you smile? What sort of stories get you "pissed off" and make your blood boil? Those things can reveal something you care deeply about.
- What do you daydream about?
- Was there an adult in your life when you were a kid you admired and liked being around? What did they do? What were they interested in that you found interesting too?
- What are some experiences that seem to repeat themselves in your life? They could indicate something that you keep drawing toward yourself.
- What were you good at when you were at school?
- What sort of things seem to come naturally to you?
- Who are your heroes, and why?

When you have answered these, take some long walks and allow your attention to wander as you contemplate.

My favourite question from Therese Rein, when interviewing people in her business where she supported people with long term injuries back into the workforce. She would ask:

"What is that thing you do, that whilst you are doing it, time seems to disappear?"

There are also questionnaires you can do on the Internet that can help you. Please do not take their findings as truth, but they may well help you. You will know when it lands.

Search for articles on the Web. Many people have lots of ideas about how to find purpose. But I suggest avoiding those who attempt to tie it to a paying career because it can limit your results.

This article by Mark Manson is clever and insightful.

https://markmanson.net/life-purpose

This article by Jack Canfield is also insightful.

https://www.jackcanfield.com/blog/finding-life-purpose/

"Peace is not something you wish for; It's something you make, something you do, something you are, and something you give away." – John Lennon

What is The Plan

Planning might not be critical, but it does create a much higher possibility of success and happiness. Benjamin Franklin was quoted, "Those who fail to plan are planning to fail".

Sir Winston Churchill is credited with another, oft-repeated, saying: "Those who fail to learn from the past are doomed to repeat it."

When we are about to initiate a significant event or make a major life change, we are stepping into territory with many "unknowns". Planning gives us a strategy to create success in our venture.

The Blindspot

Perhaps the most significant pitfall, which stops people from planning, is thinking they already know. So often, human beings tarnish their experiences by creating ideas of what it is going to be like, based on things they have seen, heard, or read.

The reality is that unless we have experienced something, we do not know.

Many changes come with working FIFO; some you will not have considered feeling like change. But change they are. If you do not plan to encounter and deal with change, you will most likely react. A reaction is often nowhere near as effective as a planned response.

I remember going on a holiday once to an island off Far North Queensland. I read all the brochures and listened to the travel agent's stories. I even spoke to some people who had been there. When we arrived, we were so disappointed with the experience that we left halfway through the holiday. It would have been more enjoyable to be at home.

On reflection, I realised that I had imagined what it would be like, and everything I read and heard just supported what I was already believing. I thought I already knew.

If I had been genuine with the situation and honest with myself, I would have admitted that this was a brand-new experience that I knew nothing of. Then I would have asked many more questions and probably would have avoided disaster and gone somewhere else, or I might still have gone there with different expectations.

So, the cold hard reality is this. If you have never worked FIFO, or have never worked in a remote place in a potentially harsh environment, or have never lived away from home for extended periods whilst working, then you do not know what it will be like. But, if you are happy to admit that to yourself, honestly admit it and own it, then you will effectively eliminate that blind spot and commence your investigations and planning.

Change Can Bring Temptations:

Many people go into FIFO because the money is excellent. Others go into it because they like the idea of more time off in a string of days. Others like the idea of the adventure.

We conducted an online survey using Survey Monkey to gather relevant data about FIFO workers, their motivations, perspectives, attitudes, and experiences. Throughout this book, we will refer back to the data we extracted from this survey.

The survey contained 38 questions and was 100% anonymous. It took, on average, 8 minutes to complete.

Following is a Question we asked the survey contributors:

Do you get to see your friends, particularly your close friends, frequently.

I have good contact with my friends.	23.44%
I am in contact with them but don't see them as much as I would like.	55.02%
I have lost contact with my friends.	8.61%
My best friends seem to be my work colleagues and I see them often.	3.35%
I don't have any good friends.	7.66%
Other (please specify)	1.91%

The Other Results included:

Rarely get to see my good friends. Most of my friend circle live interstate and I've been based in Perth for 6years now.

We're from interstate moved here in Jan hard to see mates at the moment

I choose to spend time with family, not friends

Stay in contact with siblings, parents, partner. See "friends" rarely

When we feel it is beneficial, and if we get a big enough data sample, we will provide our perspective on our analysis of the results. The above results are just interesting. If you have not yet completed the survey and would like to, here is the link:

https://www.surveymonkey.com/r/FIFO-Life

And if you enjoy the survey, I ask that you invite your friends to complete it as well. The responses provide helpful data. As I said, it is anonymous so there is no way anyone can be connected to what they write.

As you progress, changes happen. For example, there will be all the extra money. The pay packets are most often much more significant than many people are familiar with. This extra cash gives spending power and the ability to afford things previously unaffordable.

Many who do this work find themselves spending much of their money on things like cars, motorcycles, boats, home renovations, clothing, holidays, devices, partying, and many other things. Often the thought is, "I'll just get this, and then I will start saving".

Nearly 50% of our survey respondents have indicated a problem with spending. Some say they spend too much. Others say they have even gone backwards financially since starting their FIFO role.

Do you see the problem here? In such a case, the person's plan may be to start saving later rather than save now! More about this soon.

When you are out there on location, your downtime will not include the things you usually enjoy. You will make new friends, and you may want to get more involved socially. This might mean a few drinks. What stops a few drinks from turning into many drinks every night? You can afford it, right? And the booze is cheap?

And the food is plentiful, especially if you are in a camp. So what stops you from re-filling your plate every meal?

Temptations at Home Too:
And the temptation is not just for the partner who is away at work. The additional income can lead to more spending here and there. It can also lead to greater levels of indulgence in things like alcohol if boredom and loneliness become a factor.

With your "best mate" away all the time, there may well be a temptation to go out and socialize more, which can lead to over-indulgence in things you might not normally partake in regularly.

Getting a Little Self Righteous.
As soon as we start telling ourselves little stories like, "Well, I am making a big sacrifice here….." we open the door to justifications that could see us lose the farm.

As soon as you tell yourself that you are either lonely or bored, justifying your right to go out, have a drink, or spend extra money, you are no longer taking responsibility for the choices you have already made, which have led you to be exactly where you decided to be.

The cold hard reality is that there are many ways to fill in the hours you might spend alone, and perhaps the best of them all is self-improvement. This could mean a fitness program; Starting an education program; Taking on a new hobby; Learning a new language; Developing a new skill; Getting involved in some form of community service, or; Taking on a new project. There are so many productive things you can do.

Telling yourself stories to justify indulgences that were not part of your original plan means that you are no longer taking control of your life.

Here is what our survey revealed about Finances:

Question: If you did have a financial goal, how is it going?

I have stuck to it and everything is going to plan.	34.98%
It is going ok but I find I spend too much.	28.08%
Haven't started on it yet. Just enjoying having extra money.	3.45%
I have gone backwards -have been buying things I hadn't planned to.	6.90%

I can't seem to make it work.	8.87%
I never had a financial goal but would like one now.	5.42%
I never had a financial goal.	12.32%

For nearly 50% of workers, adherence to a financial goal has not happened. They obviously need more support to manifest their goals.

Imagine for a Moment...
Imagine what it would be like if:

- We elected a new national government that had no plan for the country.
- The coach of your favourite football team decided to start a new season with no plan.
- The Australian Cricket team decided to approach an Ashes Tour with no plan.
- Two of your friends decided to climb Mt Everest with no plan.
- Your parents decided to invest all their savings in a new business, with no plan.

Failing to Plan is Planning to Fail. If you simply apply for a FIFO job and then head off to start work with no plan, you may be headed for failure, or perhaps disaster. You are placing yourself at the effect of whatever might happen, around you or inside your own mind.

What is Your Inspiration for Working in a FIFO Role?

There may be many reasons for working FIFO. Some of them could be:

- The adventure of the lifestyle is appealing.
- The Money is very good, and you want to create wealth.
- The role suits your skills, and the challenge is appealing.
- It is the only job you can get that pays well enough.
- You do not like being in the city for too long.
- You want to live in Bali and need a job that will allow you to do that.
- There may be many other reasons.

Here are some Statistical Results from my FIFO Survey

My goal was to do something different and adventurous.	7.66%
It was all about lifestyle and having longer breaks between work periods.	21.05%
I wanted to enjoy a higher income so that I could enjoy a better lifestyle.	28.71%
I had a financial goal, to build wealth	19.14%
I wanted to get out of the city	1.91%
It was the best money I could earn for the skills I have	10.53%
I had no other viable options	3.35%
My mates talked me into it	0.48%
I had no goal	0.48%
Other (please specify)	6.70%

Some of the "Other" responses included:

- To get on the bigger equipment – cranes, sometimes you must go to places you don't want to go.
- To get out of the family business.
- Work life balance rather than being stuck residential in Tom price an isolated mining town.
- Excitement of challenge offshore latest technology and income and lifestyle.
  Moving up in career, learning and up skill.
- Work in the field I studied – Geology.
- Meaningful work.
  Great opportunity to work in a challenging environment with some great people.
- It was just a requirement of the work I was doing at the time - what the job entailed.
  Went FIFO to stay working for employer otherwise I would have been made redundant.
- Almost a requirement of my job - 9 years as an exploration geologist.
- Client requirements
  Looking to gain experiences to develop my career goals.

If you are in a committed relationship, does your partner have a similar inspiration for doing this work? Or are you just deciding and leaving them no choice. If it is the latter, perhaps it would be good to seek more perspectives on that decision.

Can you tell the difference between the reasons that seem deliberate and those that seem like a reaction to circumstance? This area is significant and needs to be examined. None of us likes to feel being at the effect of another person or a circumstance.

For example. Can you feel the difference between:

- I am going to work FIFO because we want to build some wealth and live debt free.
- I am going to work FIFO because I am in a bit of trouble and need the money.

The first is a forward-thinking plan. The other is a reaction to circumstances. But this does not mean the second situation is wrong, but it is more likely to lead to failure because the person is perhaps not taking deliberate charge of their life.

Once you are clear on your inspiration for doing the role, you can set about creating a plan to make it all work. But, without clear inspiration, your venture into FIFO could well be a "hit and miss" affair.

When I was 18, I had the opportunity to travel to the Bass Strait Gas Platforms to work as a Kitchen Hand. The pay was excellent. I sat down with my Mum to talk about it, and she helped me get my attention off the money and onto what I wanted.

It was November. The following March, I was to go into my second year of Physical Education, and I wanted to have a decent go at making it in the VFL. So she directed my attention to saving money, to reduce my need for part-time work during the year to dedicate my time to training.

That did it for me. I went for the role, worked hard, endured the long stints out on the rigs and saved a lot of money. The following year, I had a great season and just fell short of making it onto Fitzroy's Senior List in the VFL. But the cool thing for me is that I know I gave it my very best shot. I just was not good enough for the VFL but went on to have a rewarding career playing as an Amateur in the VAFA, making State and All Australian selection.

My Mum's wisdom paid enormous dividends for me.

So, let us get clear. What is your inspiration for working in a FIFO role?

If you are reading this now, and you are already working in FIFO, and you realise you have been working your role without a genuine sense of inspiration, it is never too late to start contemplating and come up with your "bigger why".

We explore this a little later in the chapter, "What is your inspiration for your life?"

Now or Later?

Wherever it is you are in your planning is not of concern. You can cruise along, living as you do if you wish. Or you can stop now, get some genuine planning done and start moving toward a goal. Neither is right nor wrong. It is your life s you get to choose.

But this part is essential. It does not matter where you are right now. You could be hopelessly in debt with no real vision of how you can get out of it. If you are, stop and take a breath – it's ok. The real question you must ask right now is "Where do I want to be?" or "Where do I want to get to?" The next question after that is, "Am I prepared to do what it might take to get there?" If the answer is "Yes" to both, then you are on the right track.

But - you cannot change a single thing unless you "make a decision"! Read that again!

At this point, many people falter. But, deciding means there is no going back. There are no back doors, no alternate plans, no excuses, or justifications.

When the decision is clear, and you are ready to commit, you must realise there is no turning back. Write it down, and make it known to at least one other trusted friend.

When you feel weak or begin to falter, take it out and read it again.

All outstanding achievements begin with a decision. There will be many moments of doubt. Do you think that history's ocean-faring giants like Cook, Magellan, Dampier and Hartog, those who ventured south around Cape Horn or The Cape of Good Hope, did not hit periods of doubt and indecision? Imagine those tiny boats in huge storms.

You are not human if you do not have moments of fear, self-doubt or weakness. Overcoming these things builds your self-image and your sense of self-worth. As a result, you become a stronger person.

It takes courage to succeed. Ask any successful person. But recently, in my personal exploration, I discovered something quite profound. Before I could have real courage to go after what I want, I first needed to have deep gratitude for what I have, including the opportunity to go for something bigger. It can be challenging, but we all will do well to learn gratitude for what we already have.

In the chapter on Self Development, I will give you a direction to some online resources you can use to help strengthen your willpower, which in turn builds your ability to make decisions and hold to them.

Opportunity Cost

One of the few things I clearly remember from my study of Economics in Years 11 and 12 at school was the concept of Opportunity Cost. It made sense to me, and I could feel how it applied to my life. It made decisions more straightforward.

For example, I remember going shopping for a shirt one Friday evening. I had enough money to buy one shirt. I was one of 9 kids, so my parents did not have enough money to buy us the clothes we wanted. We always had what we needed. Anything else was up to us.

So here I was. I was in a Jeans shop, and they had some super cool shirts. There were two that I wanted, but I only had the money for one. So, as I agonised over it, I realised that the "Opportunity Cost" of choosing one was missing out on the other one. Somehow that relieved the pressure, so I decided on one and always loved wearing it.

Opportunity Cost is the thing you must miss out on when you make a choice.

When I decided to pursue my Football career, the opportunity cost for me was going out drinking with my mates. I knew I could not do that, so I stopped drinking alcohol at age 18 and did not touch it again till I was 27.

What Are You Missing Out On?

If you decide to take on a FIFO Working Lifestyle, there will be opportunity costs for you to consider. First, start with your reason for doing it in the first place. Let us say, for example, you are doing it to build wealth. Then, the opportunity costs will line up for you. They might include:

- Not going to bed with the person you love every night.
- Missing being there for important events at your kids' school
- Missing football games or other sports
- Not seeing so much of your best friends
- Not being there when a friend might be in need
- Missing out on the day-to-day of being at home
- Not hanging with your kids in the evenings
- Not seeing your parents as often as you would like to
- Not walking your dog in the mornings
- There may be many others.

It would be best if you listed these down. It makes no sense to commit to the lifestyle, arrive on-site, and then realise you are missing out on all these things. Not fully considering all of these will potentially make the isolation and loneliness you may experience much worse.

The Flip Side

It is a profoundly positive step to note all the things you will gain from taking on the lifestyle, apart from your obvious, overriding inspiration or goal. These could include:

- An opportunity to make new friends
- A chance to break some bad habits
- More time on your hands to focus on getting fit again
- A chance to have quiet in the evenings so that you can study and learn new skills

- An opportunity to read more books
- The chance to start learning a new language

This change you are about to experience can be used in such a positive way. You can actually take steps to improve yourself and become a better person. You can use the space to go after things you may have long thought about.

And please take note. We are all human beings. We all make mistakes and do things that might be labelled stupid. But, no matter what you have done, it doesn't mean that is who you are for life. Every life can be resurrected and turned into something great.

If you are not proud of your past, it is important that you do not drag that negative into the present or into the future. That is who you were being back then. You do not have to be that person now or in the future.

"As it happens, with my job I do a lot of fly in fly out myself. That's because my interstate clients never agree to bringing their events to my place." **- Elliot Goblet Comedian and Funny MC.**

Chapter Summary

Failure to plan can be a trap.

The blind spot "I already know" can lead you down a dark path.

Change brings temptations. Extra cash can lead to temptation, over-spending, conflict, and a loss of control over finances.

Suddenly you can afford things you have always wanted. And the temptation to spend can be overwhelming.

There will be temptation whilst on site to drink more often than you usually would and eat more than you normally might.

Spending by the home-based partner may also get a little out of hand. Temptations can be strong.

We can get a little self-righteous about our entitlements and decisions instead of honestly looking at them.

There are positive ways you can fill in the hours you are separated from your loved ones, like study, for example.

What would life be like if the key people in our societies had no plans?

What was your inspiration for working FIFO?

What is your partner's inspiration? Are you aligned in your inspiration for the work?

Do you know the difference between a deliberate reason and a reaction to a circumstance?

It is never too late to find a bigger reason for doing what you are doing.

It does not matter where you are in your life. You can still stop, take a deep breath, and ask yourself where you want to be. That is the start of your planning.

All great achievements begin with a decision. What do you need to be able to make your decision?

Understanding opportunity cost. When you choose one thing, you will surely have to say no to something else. That is life.

What are you missing out on? Make a list of those things. Then, sit with them, and get comfortable with them.

What are the things you will gain? Make a list. Let yourself recognise them and realise where they fit into your plans.

It does not matter what you have done in the past. You can grow and improve and become an amazing person.

Life Tips from This Chapter

When you are starting out, I feel it is a wise decision to appoint a financial advisor. Make sure this person is a licensed practitioner. An accountant is a good choice as they can assist you with all your financial affairs.

Learn about cashflow budgeting. You can do a short course or read a book. I suggest you go to YouTube and sign in to SugarMamma.TV and watch her program, "My Personal Cashflow, Finance & Budgeting Secrets". It is brilliant.

If you wish, you can go to my website and request your Personal Excel Spreadsheet Cash Flow Budget Spreadsheet. Or, you can download a Budgeting App. Talk to your financial advisor about this.

Read the book "Rich Dad, Poor Dad" by Robert Kyosaki. It is very helpful. Get your kids to read it too.

Something to Consider.

As I touched on earlier, many believe that FIFO is a modern phenomenon where workers are extracted from their families in noble sacrifice to do necessary work.

Whilst part of that is true, some of it is deluded. So I invite you to consider the lives of some other people in our world.

Boarding School Kids

When I was growing up in Queensland, before we moved to Melbourne, I was amazed that my cousins went to Boarding School. Their parents lived hundreds of kilometres away, and my cousins got to see their Mum and Dad perhaps once per month.

Around Australia and the world, thousands of people spent their school years in boarding schools, learning to fend for themselves, never having any private space and having to learn to make the most of their situation.

I was once helping a friend deliver a Men's retreat, and there was a guy there whose parents were English ex-pats living in India. He was born in India, and when he was 7, they put him on a ship alone and sent him back to England to attend boarding school. He saw his parents every two years or so after that.

I will admit that whilst he was living a functional life, he had issues related to that.

Military Personnel

Most of you will know someone who is in the Military. They often go away for months at a time. Most of these trips are to inhospitable places and often place them in dangerous situations. And the pay is not that great.

GP's on Regional Postings

A shortage of Doctors and other medical professionals in regional areas means that many young Doctors spend a lot of time in regional Australia, sometimes spending months at a time because there is nobody to relieve them.

They desire to serve and care for people, and when they know there is an area without a Doctor, many put their hand up to do the job. They spend extended periods away from home.

Aid Workers

Many Aid Workers find themselves in poverty-stricken or war-torn countries for months and months on end, living in dangerous and oppressive conditions, often struggling to get access to clean water.

In some of these situations, the workers are at risk of disease and fear for their safety as corruption, crime, and tribal and political unrest surround them.

International Students

I am often amazed at the international students who travel to Australia to study. They are coming into an unfamiliar culture, often have inadequate language skills, and are away from their parents for the first time. Many do not go home for the entire duration of their course.

Some of them struggle a great deal, missing their families and the familiarity of their own culture.

These are just some of the people who are forced to leave home to live their lives. There are many, including Merchant Navy, Shearers, Truck Drivers, Buyers and Teachers.

The First Few Months

They say that it takes 21 days to break a bad habit or assume a new, good habit.

This period of change is often challenging and often when we fall prey to instinctive urges. For example, consider the person who goes on a diet, wanting to change their eating habits. They do well for six days, and then on the seventh day, for some strange and unknown reason, a compulsion, they go and "pig out" at McDonald's. All the while, their mind is telling them: It is a once-off; They have done well; The body will be shocked and will burn the extra calories anyway just digesting the meal; I'll get back on the diet tomorrow, or I am only human, and it is ok to stumble.

But the reality is that they succumbed to an instinctive need, a compulsion, that overpowered their Will, and they veered off their preferred road.

I learned during all my years of delivering The Avatar® Course that a feeling is just a feeling. Feeling hungry is just a feeling. It is not a sign that you have started down a road to death by starvation. I often use the term "starving" when I feel super hungry. But most of us in the western world are far from starving.

In fact, in March 2019, I embarked on a detox program and fasted for 14 days. For the entire time, I drank water, and four times a day, I had a drink of water with psyllium husk and bentonite clay to help clear out any built-up waste in my bowel. In addition, daily at noon, I was given a 250 ml glass of carrot juice, and at 5:30 pm, I had a 300 ml glass of clear broth, a liquid derived from boiling up potatoes.

All through it, I had periods of feeling hungry, with no access to food, so I just had to sit with it and let myself feel the feeling. And as I have experienced doing my work in Avatar Courses, a feeling is just a feeling, and if you choose to allow yourself to feel it without resisting it, it passes. And so too did the hunger. So I survived the 14 days pretty easily.

So, we all have feelings, urges, desires and yearnings. But we also have Will Power. Saying "No" to all these things will strengthen our Will. It is hard to change something. The old urges keep wanting to drag you back. But your Will is stronger.

Human Will is Amazing

I was once out driving a couple of hundred kilometres northwest of Perth with a young guy who had done several years of Military Service in the Australian Army. We were talking about Will, and he shared something quite profound with me. He said that when a soldier comes back from a prolonged Military Exercise, or even a Tour of Duty, they have a problem. They have lost their capacity to "make a decision".

He shared that when they are away, they are following orders 24/7. Someone else is making all the decisions, and they simply must obey orders. So by the time they get back to Townsville, they are dependent on someone else's direction. He went on to say that often these soldiers could be found in a supermarket, standing staring at a shelf, unable to decide which brand of a product they would buy. He said it could take a couple of weeks to "quarantine them" and get them back to a state where they could function again.

This information was mind-blowing for me. I wonder how many people have allowed their job, their urges and desires, or even their need for acceptance, become their "army". How many have lost the capacity to decide because their circumstances completely control their life? I imagine it is a lot.

Having a strong will is essential to improving or changing your life. It is the driving force to your imagined future.

Avatar® and ReSurfacing® are registered trademarks of Star's Edge, Inc.

Strengthening Your Will

There are many ways to strengthen your Will. Perhaps the easiest I know of is to use the exercises you would learn in an Avatar Re-Surfacing Workshop. ReSurfacing runs for two days and can be life-changing. I would recommend the entire Avatar® Course to any person who wants to make their life better. It gives you the skills to navigate this world and to create what you really want.

You can explore it more here at www.avataroceania.com.

If the Avatar training is not your immediate choice, you can strengthen your Will by taking on challenges that scare you a little; that put you at risk of failure. So exercise is always a good one.

For example, You might decide to compete in a 10km Fun Run, yet you have not done any running for ten years. You know it will be hard and that it will put you through a lot of pain and discomfort. Good for you!

To start, you would need to pick your event and then state your intention to somebody who will hold you accountable. Then you will need a training program and some guidance. It is good to spend some time and money with a personal trainer and get yourself a program, along with some additional exercises to reduce your injury risk.

It is not the purpose of this book to discuss exercise physiology or training programs, but you must do the work once you have the program. So, many times each week, you will have to do your training. And this is where your Will either kicks in or leaves you sitting on the sofa.

You will be forced to overcome all your laziness, excuses, urges, desires, and fears to get up and do it. And you will probably have to do the same tomorrow and the next day. But as time progresses, your Will gets stronger.

The key to this is the decision to act. "I think I will go out training soon" is not a decision. It is a phenomenon somewhere between a self-soothing fantasy and the mind talking shit.

But when you say to yourself, "It's training time, and I am going now", and you stand up and walk out the door and out onto the street and start running, well, that is a decision. And you must do it every day if you want to achieve your goal.

On another occasion when I saw Tommy Hafey out training and stopped for a chat. I asked, "What time did you bounce out of bed this morning

Tommy?" His response took me back a little. "Bounce?" he said, "It was a 6 round fight." He went on to tell me he had to drive 4 hours to get home last night and did not get to bed till 1:00 am. So, when his alarm went off, the mental war began. His mind gave him countless reasons why he did not need to go today. "The protests were deafening," he told me, but then I heard that old familiar voice from somewhere back in the rear, "Get outta bed ya lazy bastard!"

We often think other people have it easy. But that is a mistake; They are all human beings just like us. We all have our strengths and our weaknesses, our urges, and our desires.

I recall an incredible story from the great Sebastian Coe. It was at the height of his running career and his legendary rivalry with countryman Steve Ovett. It was Christmas Day, freezing cold with snow and sleet outside. He went for a training run in the morning and set about enjoying Christmas with his family. At lunch, he felt uncomfortable and irritable. After some time, he realised it was because he did not feel he had trained enough that day, so he went and changed and headed out to run another 20 kilometres. When he came back, he was able to enjoy his Christmas. Years later, he shared the story with Ovett, and Ovett responded by saying, "Did you only go out twice that day?"

You Need to Re-decide Every Day

Here is the bottom line. If you want to change and create something new, you have to decide every day, sometimes several times a day. It is a good thing to write your goals down and read them daily. Then decide you are going to do what is needed today to get you closer to that goal.

You will have bad days, but they are not the end of the world. They are just a bad day.

My good friend William White told me of his childhood and teenage years where, as a kid with dyslexia, he struggled at school. He was always in trouble, sometimes, severe trouble, like the day the Police arrested him after burning down a shed in the neighbourhood.

When his Mum came to pick him up and take him home, she put her arms around him and said what she always said when he was in trouble, "It's just been a bad day, darling".

Putting that label on the experience probably released him from it, giving him the chance to start again tomorrow. William went on to become a profoundly successful artist and humanitarian.

Keep deciding every day, and let the bad days be just that, "Just a bad day!"

The First Three Months is Crucial

Whether you are just starting in FIFO or have been doing it for a long time, the next three months are crucial.

If you want to make things work, the next three months is so important. But first, you will need to write down your starting date. What date do you start work, or what date do you want to start overhauling your life?

Once you have your start date, you can quickly write down the last day or your next three months. By that date, you can have a lot of things either "in motion" or sorted.

There must be a start point. Things do not just happen. It is up to you to make them happen, and you must start somewhere.

There are many things I imagine you could wish to change in the next three months, so I will cover a few of them.

Money

Perhaps you need to save money. So you will need a savings goal. That is not too hard to work out. Write down all your costs for a month, including a reasonable amount for food expenditure. Once you subtract that from your income, you then know how much you will have remaining. Multiply that amount by three, and you have your savings target for the first three months.

For example:

Rent or Mortgage	2,500
Electricity and Gas	200
Other House Bills, eg rates	120

Insurances	200
Telephone and Internet	190
School Fees	500
Weekly Grocery Shopping x 4.3 for a month	1,075
Pocket Money – You, your partner, and kids	800
Car Payments	420
Credit Card Payments	200
Household Petty Cash – emergency items	200
Petrol and other Transport Costs like Trains	150
Other Costs	100
Total Monthly Costs	6,725
Monthly Net Income Received (You and partner)	9,500
Surplus for Savings	2,775
Over 3 months	8,325

This table is just a basic example, but it allows you to see what is possible. For example, based on the figures above, this person could have enough money to purchase an investment property at the end of a year.

As an added support, you could open another bank account that you cannot access unless you visit the branch and transfer the amount you expect to save into that account as soon as your wage deposit arrives.

A plan like this requires total commitment. Without it, you weaken, break your own rules, and finish up collapsing and abandoning it altogether.

It means that over this time, you would not:

- Buy clothes
- Use a Credit Card
- Buy any toys
- Have a "big night out".
- Have a punt.

Now, if any of these things are important to you, they should be included in your budget. But, again, we are not talking about being draconian here, just disciplined.

I want to inspire you to create a plan and then stick to it. When you do, your self-respect and self-confidence will soar.

Exercise and Nutrition

You may have decided to improve your health and fitness. This goal will require exercise and a supportive nutritional plan.

I once heard a talk by Yogi Satchidananda. He talked about committing to change your life. In it, he said, "When you are starting out on a great journey, it is important to start from where you are now and not from where you think you should be."

This is wise advice. It does not matter how unfit you are. Once you start exercising, you will begin to get fitter. I have seen so many people who decide to start exercise, but they are so much in denial about how they have let themselves go that they start with unrealistic expectations.

The result is that it is sickeningly hard and completely unenjoyable, and they feel like a failure and give up - such a bad strategy.

You are better off starting at a low level and accomplishing the task. Then, if it was too easy, increase it next session. Finally, you will find that place where the challenge is adequate to stimulate improvement. And you will enjoy it.

It is good to consult a personal trainer and ask them to help you put a plan together.

When it comes to diet, radical overhauls are often not a great idea. Instead, you must choose your plan based on your common sense and not your bravado.

First, make sure you are drinking enough water, then look at how you usually eat. Then, how can you modify it in a way that is doable? Again, consulting a trainer or a nutritionist is a wise move.

Keeping Your Relationship Strong

Later in the chapter, "Taking Care of Home Base", I explore various topics relating to keeping things running smoothly and in harmony, back at home whilst you are away working.

Strong and enduring relationships do not just happen. Just because you fall in love with someone, and they with you, does not mean that they will put up with difficulties, let down, disappointment, absence, disconnection, and disinterest for an extended time.

Relationships take effort.

What are the things your partner loves? What are the things your partner does not like? How much support does your partner need? What can you do to add quality to your partner's life, even though you are a long way away?

Sometimes a small gift in the mail, or a loving message by text, or just a note to let them know you are thinking of them, or how much you appreciate them, can be so powerful.

Do not get lazy in your relationship.

A relationship is a lot like fitness. You can train hard for a period to create the fitness level you want. But if you stop training, you will lose it.

Remember how hard you worked to woo this person and get them into your life. You must keep wooing them, keep reminding them of who you really are and why they love you so much. Many people become too comfortable and then wonder why their partner is no longer as loving to them as they once were.

If you would like your partner to be loving toward you, you must consistently be loving toward your partner. When you are talking with them, they need to feel they are the only person in the world that you want to be with at that time.

Digital Distractions

Devices are not suitable when you are with your loved ones. Put them away. You could try creating an agreement with your partner and perhaps your family that all devices are put away at certain times.

When your device is handy, you will have attention on it and not on your partner or loved one. That sucks. Nobody enjoys feeling second best, especially to a phone or tablet.

Good Sex

Be deliberate about sex. I talk about this more later. Many people get lazy in their relationships, and their sex becomes routine, which means it is not exciting.

The trick is not to allow sex to be something you "squeeze in" before going to sleep. It needs to be much more than that. Set time aside and make it happen with connection, patience, and togetherness.

Sharing Your Intimacy

I will cover this in more detail later too. But do not separate your intimacy when you are away. Whatever you like to do whilst you are away, share it with your partner.

For the "New Comers"

Whilst I cover this later in the book, it is crucial to get a plan in place with your partner if you have one. How are you going to make it all happen? For example:

- Make your roster clear so that your family know when you are coming and going.
- What plans can you put in place to make a valuable contribution when you get home. For example, mowing lawns, cleaning, taking over the cooking to give your partner a break, spending quality time with your kids to give your partner some time out, etc.
- How often are you going to communicate while you are away? What times are you going to do that?
- Have a clear conversation with your partner and your kids. What are the things you find hardest about being away? And

what do they find hardest about you not being there? Everyone needs to be heard. You might not be able to fix those things but have the conversation and listen.

- You are in a perfect position because you are starting out, to align with your partner and set some exciting financial goals.
- As you move forward, keep having the conversations. Neither you nor your partner must ever end up in a rut, where you are enduring things that are not how you would like them. In this state, resentment builds and is soon followed by conflict.

For the "Old Timers"

Over the next three months, you have an opportunity to repair your bad habits and set to work on fixing the things that are not working too well.

Everyone can easily fall into a rut in their life. A routine can become the usual, and eventually, we can find ourselves living a habitual pattern, which I reckon is probably a rut.

When nothing changes, there are no challenges. Without challenges, we do not have to grow and evolve. Unfortunately, nature does not take too kindly to a "no growth" zone.

So, even if you have been doing this work for years, you cannot create harm by stepping back and looking at how you are doing it.

If you are in a committed relationship, and/or if you have kids, perhaps you could explore it. Consider the following:

- Ask your family how they view what you do, especially when you come home. How do they think you could do it better? Invite them to be brutally honest with you. Avoid taking offence.
- Are there things you could be doing whilst home to add more value to your family's life?
- Are there things you could be doing around the house to make your home more valuable, inviting or nurturing?
- If you started growing vegetables, could you team up with your family to have them care for your gardens while you are away?

- Are there things needed in the community that you could contribute to, like Sports Clubs, community groups, school committees etc.?
- Are there problems and challenges in your community that everyone seems to ignore because nobody has a solution, like disaffected youth? What might you be able to do to help out?

All these things, which I have no doubt some of you already do, add value to your life because they add value to other people's lives.

There is another piece to this. If you are a FIFO old-timer, and you have everything working smoothly, at work and home, what mentoring can you provide to the new people to help them get their life organised and functioning smoothly? You probably have a great deal of wisdom to share.

A Note of Caution:
1. If you are mentoring, try to refrain from telling people how they should do it.
2. Listen to them and share the challenges you faced and how you went about overcoming them.
3. Ask them about their challenges and ask them to come up with ideas about how they can overcome them. As you mentor them, you are holding a safe space and giving them the confidence and support they need to solve their problems.

Chapter Summary

It takes 21 days to create, break or change a habit.

Instinctive needs, urges and compulsions make things challenging when you are trying to change things up.

Feelings are just feelings. We do not have to respond to them.

We all have feelings, urges, desires and yearnings. But we also have willpower.

Soldiers who have been on tour or in a military exercise for an extended time, and operating under orders, lose their will. They cannot make decisions.

Strengthening your Will: The Avatar Course ReSurfacing workshop and associated exercises are extremely powerful.

Take on challenges that scare you a little, like Train for a Fun Run, or Read 2 books in a month.

Pick your challenge carefully. Then tell some people you are going to do it. Declare it publicly.

Overcome all your laziness, excuses, desires, urges, and fears.

Getting out of bed can sometimes be the hardest thing – but it is the gateway to success.

Re-deciding every single day is important. Stay fully connected to and committed to your decision.

Sometimes you just have a bad day.

The first three months are crucial. Write down your start date. Then calculate the end date…3 months later.

A plan for saving money. What are your expenses, weekly and monthly? Excel Spreadsheet.

What is your monthly surplus? Multiply this by three, and you have a savings goal.

Having a plan, an additional bank account, to put money out of reach.

Create a spending plan and stick to it. Keep extra money out of your reach.

When it comes to exercise, start from where you are now.

With diet and exercise, create reasonable and achievable goals.

Get advice and guidance from Personal Trainers and/or Nutritionists.

Strong and enduring relationships do not just happen. They take effort.

How well do you know your partner? What do they like and dislike?

Remind them you are thinking of them. Do not get lazy.

Remember the effort you put in to attract this person. You cannot stop now.

Avoid all forms of digital distractions when you are with your partner.

Make efforts to create time for good, connected sex. Do not allow it to become "run of the mill".

For the newcomers: You can get things right from the start.

For the old-timers, it is never too late to change something and make things better.

Life Tips from This Chapter

Read the great Australian Biography, "A Fortunate Life" by A.B. Facey. This is a wonderful story about life, written by man who suffered some terrible experiences on his journey. It is a beautiful book.

This talk on YouTube from Admiral William McRaven, a University of Texas Commencement Address in 2014. It is uplifting, funny and brilliant.

https://www.youtube.com/watch?v=pxBQLFLei70

Set yourself a goal or two for something that you must discipline yourself to do each day. Just take on one thing. When it becomes more routine, add another. For example.

- Get up at a certain time each day.
- Go to bed at a certain time each day.
- Do 15 push-ups when you get out of bed.
- Stand under a cold shower for 30 seconds at the end of your morning shower.
- Walk for 20 minutes following your evening meal.
- Read 10 pages of a book every day.
- Cut your sugar intake down over 2 weeks to zero.
- Meditate for 10 minutes before going to sleep.
- Stop drinking alcohol from Monday to Friday.

I am sure you can think of many more.

Good Cashflow versus Wealth

Starting a new job that pays you more than three thousand dollars per week does not make you wealthy. It just means you have excellent cash flow.

Good cash flow only remains good if the amount of money coming in continues to be more than what is going out. One person may have good cash flow when earning $200 per week whilst another might have terrible cash flow whilst earning $20,000 per week.

It seems that a relevant definition for financial wealth in this modern market economy is "Owning an abundance of assets that continue to grow in value and produce regular income, over and above what one needs to fund the desired lifestyle".

Hence, this would mean a truly wealthy person is a person who owns substantial assets and who gets to choose how they live without any form of financial restriction and without reducing the value of those assets.

This is probably what many would define as financial freedom.

A person who does not own substantial assets, yet may have a substantial income, might feel they are wealthy, but they are limited by the duration of the role that provides the income. Therefore, they are not rich, just "cashed up".

There is an unkind term used in the mining industry to define people who have not come from wealth and find themselves in a highly paid employment role and like spending sprees. They are referred to as Cubs, which is short for "Cashed Up Bogans".

Good cash flow, however, can be a wonderful pathway to establishing genuine wealth.

Where do You Stand?

Former West Coast Eagles Vice Captain John Annear and I discuss the FIFO situation a lot. John is a well-known Perth Physiotherapist, and he is one of those men that cares a lot. He often talks to young players potentially moving into the AFL ranks and advises them about money management.

His advice is wise and sound. First, he asks them what their mates are doing for a job. Often it is something like "Apprentice this" or "Junior that", and he asks what their mates are earning in their career. Once they arrive at that figure, he then tells them that they should aim to live off that amount and have the rest of their money put away in savings for them.

In my first full-time job, I was working in a health club in Melbourne. I was clearing $200 per week. Each week when I received my pay, I divided the cash up into a set of containers I kept in a drawer. I had containers for:

- Rent $30
- Food and Bills $60
- Car $20
- Entertainment $30
- Clothes $20
- Savings. $40

I was not earning much, but I could still save some money. It was tempting to spend that savings amount, but I put it in the bank, so I always had money for Christmas. I earned similar money to my mates, so we all made the most of our recreational cash and did not over-spend.

Earning more money than your friends should not be your chance to feel better than them or give yourself special status in your friendship group. It is just money.

Money among friends is not a competition. If you earn more than your mates, it does not make you better or superior to them. You just get paid differently for your work. There are upsides and downsides to everything. Thinking you are better and showing off your money is not cool. It will see you lose your friends.

A fool and his money are soon parted.

Spending on Your Mates

During my research for this book, I met young men who felt that they should spend money on their friends simply because they had it and their mates did not.

This single topic could be a book in itself. However, when we look at our motivations for things we do in life, all sorts of things arise including, Love, care, approval, disapproval, opportunism, advantage, payback, anger, entitlement, service, creative expression, and many others.

I always found an uncomfortable moment when going on a date. Should I pay, or should we split the bill? I certainly do not mind paying, but then I feel I am perhaps disempowering my date, so in a way, I am not respecting her by paying. But, on the other hand, one could argue that by paying, I am saying, you cannot afford this, but I can. So, it was always this weird moment where I would be waiting to see if she made a move to make a payment.

In the end, I realised how crazy it was and started having the conversation well beforehand. I realised that my date partner probably felt the same.

I grew up in Pubs and am so familiar with the concept of a shout. When two or more men drank together, they would take turns buying the drinks. There was an unwritten rule that kept everything fair. It taught me something. If I did not want to drink at the same pace as my friends, I drank with them but chose not to be part of "the shout".

Over time, I watched many different types drinking together, including pensioners with workers, boss types with workers; pensioners with boss types; elite athletes with their mates. The rules never changed. If you were in a shout, you took your turn. It never mattered how much money someone had. When it was your shout, you paid.

It was always a silent rule that kept things in order.

How then did we get to where a bloke feels he should pay because he earns more than his mates? There are a couple of things to look at here.

First, your mates probably do not expect you to shout. If they do, then you need to help them with that. That sort of entitlement will bring them a great deal of unhappiness in their lives. It is just not on.

If you feel the urge to shout everyone, you are probably just showing off and using your money to dominate your mates. That is not cool and will likely create jealousy. Your friendships will not last long.

I must admit to being stunned sometimes when a bloke tells me he has had a night out and "dropped a grand". I am not sure why anyone would do that. But, if that is your choice, I wish you well.

If you are one of those people who loses a bit of control when you go out, I have a piece of advice for you. Take cash and leave your cards at home.

Remember, a fool and his money are soon parted.

Learning to Save and to be Frugal

The early Australian Immigrants, many from Italy, Greece, Lebanon, and many displaced Jewish people from Europe, came to Australia and created wealth.

At the time, the post-war economies were booming as the world re-built itself. Many of these "new" Australians had come from humble existences, and they continued with their way of life in Australia. I am not sure if it was planned or simply carrying on a normal lifestyle, but these families turned their back yards into small farms, producing substantial amounts of their own food and working hard at labour intensive jobs.

Many of these people saved everything they could, and over time, they invested in real estate. As a result, many of my friend's parents gave them a house when they got married. It was amazing to see that people who lived on a single wage from an unskilled job could create the way they did.

Saving is one of those things that seems to have vanished from the discussion. As a kid, we were encouraged to save. But somewhere in the late 70's or 80's things changed, and I am guessing it was the introduction of the credit card. Buy it now and pay for it later!

We shifted from a mentality of save for it or use lay-by to get it now and worry about the bill later. And the banks have used this system to build profound wealth as willing consumers happily fork out interest rates well above 20%.

Perhaps our competitive nature kicked in here too. "If my mate or my brother can have a nice car, then why can't I?"

Modern Day Saving:

Modern Day saving is more about investing in something. Most often, it is property or shares. Whilst the latter can be somewhat speculative and has been known to be the source of crippling losses when markets crash, the former has been a natural playground for stable growth.

One of the challenges faced by many are that the property market has experienced such incredible growth over time that the average person is finding it more and more challenging to raise the funds needed to get started.

Further, there are many property projects presented in glossy presentations that carry huge risks. The market has become much more complex, with many traps and pitfalls. For example, many people have been caught out buying brand new apartments in city side residential towers that plummeted in value soon after acquisition.

Often, people are taking advice from Sales professionals instead of educating themselves and making informed decisions.

However, the advice I receive is that a suitable investment in property can be both sound and wealth-creating over the long term.

I have seen staggering levels of stupidity in markets where property values have skyrocketed, and cashed-up and unwitting investors have paid hugely inflated prices for homes, only to be devastated by a market crash. Take Gladstone, for example, on the central Queensland Coast.

When the Gladstone Port and the Gas Plants were being built, massive workforces came to town, and property supply was limited. So, prices rose, and people kept paying. Finally, when all the work was completed, and the workers left town, some were left holding properties they could not sell. Some properties, purchased for over $700k, were not worth more than $300k.

If you wish to build wealth by investing in property, I suggest doing a course or two, learning the fundamentals of the market, or seeking a reputable Buyers' Advocate who will provide wise guidance.

Purchasing shares can be little better than gambling on a racehorse. There are many opportunities for quick wealth, and many will speculate. However, this is a game that one should play only if you have a deep understanding of the market and how to make gains whether the market is rising or falling.

Investing in a single stock just because someone you know said it is "a good thing" is foolhardy and reckless.

If you are serious about building wealth using the Stock Market, I urge you to engage a reputable broker.

The Urge to Spend

Just this morning, I was faced with an enticing advertisement on my iPad. The product looked interesting, and I followed the links. And guess what, I almost made the purchase. But then I stopped myself and asked myself a straightforward question. "Do I need this thing, or do I just want it?" The answer was that I did not need it. So, I aborted the purchase.

But who governs us? When we were kids, we tormented our parents to buy the things we wanted. It is staggering the lengths we would go to, to get what we wanted. So, I have an exercise for you.

Go somewhere and watch people. Watch a child, or even better, a young teenager, when they want their parent to buy something. They go to all manner of lengths to convince, seduce, manipulate, plead and guilt-trip the parent into making the purchase. At that moment, you can see the "all-out-attack" on the parent.

While the teenager is doing this, they are sitting in a fascinating viewpoint. They feel entirely entitled to do what they are doing and will not stop till they either create success or it becomes unsafe to proceed. This "entitlement" is a product of the modern era. Advertisers are geniuses at helping us to feel entitled.

Now take a good look at yourself. When did you last make a purchase that you felt fully entitled to make but did not need it? I reckon our minds do to us the exact thing the teenager is doing to their parent.

Bringing our spending under control takes a lot of self-discipline. And some just do not have that discipline.

I remember a friend who told me about his daughter, who was always short of money. One day, she wanted to change bedrooms in the house, so he volunteered to assist her. He went for the shoes first and gathered only the shoes on the floor in her bedroom. There were 25 pairs. He said he was afraid to open the closet.

This situation is a case of "Money burning a hole in your pocket".

Wants Versus Needs

As you will read later in this book, Human Beings need very few things to survive. Air, Water, Food, Shelter, Community, and something worthwhile to do, make up the list. Everything else can be classified as a "Want".

When "Wants" become "Needs", we can easily lose perspective and find ourselves over-committed. Consider the following:

- Needing to have the absolute best car because a few of your mates have one.
- Needing the latest Mobile Phone when the one you have already is working perfectly
- Needing a Bloke's Den at home complete with a "Mega" entertainment system and bar fridge.
- Needing a Motor Bike so you have something to do on your days off.
- Needing a whole new wardrobe.....

There is nothing wrong with any of these. However, if they are impulse purchases or not part of a plan, you are not controlling your spending.

Spending

It is easy to allow your spending to get out of control. There are so many things to buy, and so many of them seem to be inconsequential. Have you ever heard yourself say, "It's only ten bucks!"

But it all adds up. For example, I sat with a young lady last year who complained she had no money and felt she was buying too many clothes. So, I surprised her when I asked her how many coffees she has per day.

She said she has at least two, seven days per week. That is $4 per coffee, at least $56 per week. Some days she has more, so let us round it off to $70 per week on coffees. Her head nearly fell off when I told her she was spending $3,500 per year on coffees.

$4 does not seem like much at all till you add them all together.

These "little spends" are your money drains. They are like a proverbial hole in your pocket. So, it is a good idea to sit down and write down all of these "little spends" and see how they are affecting you. Here are some ideas:

- Coffees
- Soft Drinks
- Alcoholic Drinks with friends
- Snacks
- Meals away from home
- Toll fees
- Parking
- Cigarettes
- Many others

What can you put in place to remove these? I had a friend who saved a small fortune by making extra dinner each night and then taking it to work as a packaged lunch, as you do onsite with crib. In two years, he saved enough to put down a deposit on an investment property.

Companies and Cash Reserves

Great companies create cash reserves that they can call upon in times of need. Such resources provide stability and power. The company can survive market fluctuations, challenges like a pandemic and take new directions without fear of becoming unstable. Apple, for example, famously has over $1 trillion in the bank.

It is also beneficial for people to have savings. When you have cash in the bank, you can settle, knowing that you will be ok if challenging times visit. The best path to creating savings is through discipline. Anyone who has a regular wage can save. Anyone with a large regular wage should save.

A man I know very well worked hard in his trade. He had a relationship that was not ideal and had two daughters. Without much notice, his partner left him and the girls for another man and moved away for years. He took responsibility and cared for his girls whilst working at his job.

Again, without much warning, his ex-partner arrived back and wanted to take her daughters. She went to court and won, and he was left heartbroken, only able to see his girls every second week. So, he put his head down and worked hard and saved. Eventually, his daughters completed school and moved to Melbourne, where he was living, and he was able to provide both girls with a house.

He was not earning a huge wage, but he did all the overtime he could and kept his eye on his goal. As a result, his daughters now live stable lives and are deeply grateful to their Dad's love and dedication.

Chapter Summary

Aligning yourself with your best friends is wise. Learn to live off the lower amount of what they earn. Save the rest.

Simple budgets can work incredibly well.

Earning more money than your friends does not mean you are better than them.

A fool and his money are soon parted.

Handle your urges to pick up the bill for your friends just because you can.

When you pay, are you disempowering the other person.

You do not have to be part of the "shout".

If you are one of those people who loses a bit of control over your spending when you go out, take cash and leave your cards at home. Put yourself on a spending limit.

When Credit Cards arrived on the scene in the '80s, saving seemed to lose its popularity. Instead, buy now, pay later became the new trend.

Sometimes our purchases may come from our need to compete with others.

Taking advice from the person selling the investment is foolhardy at best.

If you are to become an investor, either educate yourself or employ the services of a trusted, independent advisor.

There are lessons to be learned from Gladstone in Queensland following the completion of major construction projects.

Taking "Tips" on the stock market is no better than taking "tips" on the racetrack.

An important question: "Do I really need this purchase, or do I just want it?"

Take time out to watch a teenager or an older child in a shopping centre tormenting their parent to make a purchase they want. Realise, this is what you do to yourself.

Bringing our spending under control takes a lot of self-discipline. And some do not have that discipline.

Does money burn a hole in your pocket?

Understand the difference between a "Want" and a "Need". When "Wants" become "Needs", we lose perspective.

Advertisers are waiting around every corner to seduce you into parting with your money. Spending is so easy, especially on a card. You do not even notice the balance dwindling.

Two coffees per day can equal nearly $3,000 per year.

Your "little spends" are your money drains. Sit down and write them down. See them for what they are.

Small sacrifices can bring big rewards.

Having money in savings gives you stability in your life.

Life Tips from This Chapter

Create a cashflow budget for yourself and check it every 2 to 3 days.

When you go out for a night, take a set amount of cash and leave your cards at home.

Set yourself a Savings Target and reward yourself when you meet your progressive targets.

Avoid hanging out with friends who are wasteful with their money, spending on expensive drinks and drugs.

Find a financial mentor and check in regularly.

If you have a partner, plan together and keep each other accountable.

Sign up to Sugar Mamma TV on YouTube. Canna Campbell is brilliant. She gives amazing advice that is simple to follow. Follow her on Instagram too and sign up for her podcasts.

If your finances are completely out of control, visit My Budget at https://www.mybudget.com.au/ and start a conversation.

What is Your Inspiration for Your Life?

How do You Find Genuine Inspiration for your life?

One day a few years ago, I was sitting with a friend in a course. He had driven up to Melbourne from Geelong that morning during peak hour, and it had taken him 2 hours. He said to me, "People do it every day, five days a week. And then they do it again in the afternoon to get home."

His story struck a chord with me on several levels. But first, I have to say that people are free to choose where they live, where they work and how they go to and from work. Second, I wish to make it clear that I am not taking a position of a lofty critic in writing this. It is a fascinating topic to explore.

Many who are reading this are familiar with the frenetic wind down leading into Christmas. It is incredible to watch as everyone's stress builds and builds to a peak, then they come to a screeching halt and try to get centred for Christmas Day with relatives.

When I was growing up, I thought the wind down to Christmas was meant to be a gradual and gentle progression. How things have changed.

I wonder if we need to re-write the 12 days of Christmas.

On the 12th day of Christmas my true love sent to me:

- 12 hours of frantic shopping
- 11 budgets hammered
- 10 sales staff yelled at
- 9 coffees guzzled
- 8 emails per minute
- 7 wines too many
- 6 headache tablets
- 5 late nights each week
- 4 falling stocks
- 3 stressed friends
- 2 leads are duds

- And a script for anxiety meds.

So, if things are not how you would like them to be, perhaps it is time to explore. What would you prefer?

Often at this point, people say to me, "Oh, I would rather travel!" Great, cash in your super and do it. But travel for most is a temporary thing. Most of us need to work to survive, to be doing something worthwhile. And I do not just refer to income. Without something worthwhile to do, we do not thrive. We become like a plant that loses its access to sunlight. It withers and dies.

What would you rather be doing with your life? Changing jobs is a bit like changing the furniture. Sooner or later, you realise it is still the same house, in the same street. So what do you want to do? If you have no idea, that is ok. But please, I do not want to ask this question 12 months from now, and you still do not have an answer. That would be a tragedy.

I believe that we are all born with a spark of inspiration. I may not be right about that, but I sense that it is close to accurate. Some discover it early and go after it. Some realise it, struggle to see how to make a living from it, then set it aside and focus on creating a career that pays a reliable wage.

Others find it later in life. And then some have never even considered the possibility of such a thing. And finally, some have never heard of the concept of life purpose yet are fully engaged in living their purpose. You often find these among Police Officers, Nurses and other service personnel.

So, if you are one of those who is battling boredom or "same shite different year" syndrome, and you crave the clarity to find out what your true purpose is, then perhaps it is time to start exploring. Maybe it is time to take another look and get a little more interested.

Taking on a FIFO role often gives you that time to more deeply contemplate and explore your existence. So, whilst you stow away a bit of a financial nest egg, you might very well discover what it is you do want to do this lifetime.

One of the challenges is all the beliefs and ideas crammed into our minds about how we should be or what we should be doing. For example, walking away from a secure job with a good pay packet is madness, right? I would argue that if you hate it, it is madness staying in there.

One day you will draw your last breath. Will you look back on your life with deep satisfaction or regret, or will your head be filled with justifications?

Sometimes, to get to the core of your own unique inspiration, you need first to clear out all the mental noise and find out what is actually there. This process may take hours, and it may take weeks. I cannot tell you for sure. But if you are going to get there, having some effective tools will help you awaken who you really are and connect you with your purpose. And along the way, you might sort out a few other issues too.

Some use meditation. Others use long, quiet walks during which they can contemplate many things. The first thing to look at is all the beliefs and ideas that keep you bound up, the ideas of how you should be, of what is expected of you or what you believe other people think. These are all just ideas and beliefs. None of them is likely to be cold, hard, life facts.

I sense that one of the reasons we love our long-standing music idols is that they chose a different path. They picked up their guitars and headed out on the road. I remember an interview with American Guitar Legend and Eagles Band Member Joe Walsh. When asked why he dropped out of university, he replied, "I figured I did not need a degree to stay up all night!"

Here are a couple of clues for you. The first, which I find most powerful, is that an authentic life purpose always seems to be something that will benefit another person or people somehow.

Following is an article I wrote in 2018 after being involved in a magnificent Civil Engineering project with the John Holland Group in Melbourne.

What Can We Learn from Catastrophes to make Working Lives Better?

Catastrophes often bring out the very best in people. When the needs of others are so urgent and profoundly obvious, something seems to awaken in the human heart, and great works are achieved.

I look at the destruction of some locations following Earthquakes, for example. I was in Christchurch following the quakes there, and I looked around with helplessness. I thought to myself, "How is this mess ever going to be cleaned up, and how will this all be restored? Who will do it?"

But it gets done.

What is more, in the hours and days following the disaster, people voluntarily work hundreds of hours, going long stretches without sleep in difficult and profoundly stressful circumstances, saving lives, restoring some order, and creating somewhere safe for those affected to find comfort.

Even the toughest unionist has no attention on time, working conditions, or breaks during these times, and nobody is interested in slowing down to prolong the work.

During such times, we humans are driven by our hearts, our primary care for others, and our most profound empathy for the suffering of others. These are some of the finest qualities of human beings.

So how do we help to bring these qualities alive in our day-to-day workplace, where people naturally come more from a place of care for others than from self-interest. But, again, self-interest is a common and sometimes helpful trait of being human. But, there are also times when it is the roadblock that stops alignment, cooperative acts and strong and positive workplace cultures.

How do we bring out these qualities that inspire good people to bring their "A" game to their work, give for the sake of giving, and enjoy the adventure of being part of something good?

Not long ago, I had the opportunity to work with a large team preparing to take on a considerable challenge. But, unfortunately, everyone was stressed and resisting the event.

The event was an extended occupation spanning a couple of months where a major suburban train line was to be closed, a massive amount of earth moved, and new train lines routed underneath three roads, two of them busy thoroughfares. New train stations had to be built as well.

This was to be a huge project involving over 1000 employees with shifts going around the clock. Therefore, the allocated time frame could not blow out because the disruption would be significant.

When I addressed them, we looked at what was going to happen, what the outcome would be, and how it would affect the community moving forward in the future. We talked about the incredibly positive impact of their work for future generations and the positive impact on families, on parents' ability to spend more time with their kids and on the general welfare of the community at large.

We took a detailed exploration of the ongoing benefit of the project, the impact on the city, the state and the communities most closely affected. Finally, we looked at what would happen if the project did not go ahead. As we progressed, the team began to feel the profound awesomeness of their project and the legacy their efforts would leave. It was truly amazing to feel the collective shift in perspective.

The attitude shifted from one of fear and stress to one of positivity and excitement. This was going to be a landmark event in the lives of many of these workers.

The team completed the project nearly two days early and under budget. As I drive past it now, I shake my head as I realise what this group of incredible people achieved.

I spoke to the Project Manager, and he reported that it was indeed an extraordinary experience. He said they were greeted by incredibly warm community engagement all through the event. He told me, "We became the city's number one tourist attraction. Daily we had so many people gathering at the fence to see what was happening. As personnel walked around the site, they would be stopped by regular citizens asking what was happening on an aspect of the project or what a piece of machinery was for. The interest and curiosity were off the chart. Even though there was extraordinary disruption, there were no complaints, and everyone enjoyed the task. We were all moved by the support we felt."

Throughout the project, there were no complaints at all, and just two slightly negative tweets. The bus service used to replace the trains carried over 800,000 passengers between the two points where the line had been closed.

I wonder what they might have experienced if they had gone into the project with their heads down, thinking it would be awful, and stressed by what lay ahead?

Sometimes I feel we lose sight of what we are doing with our work. As a result, we forget our impact on people's lives when we do our job well. And if management and leadership lose this connection, the workforce most certainly will.

I wonder if you have ever taken time out to look at what your organisation is doing? Have you asked these questions?

- Who does this project serve?
- Who are the immediate beneficiaries?
- How will the community benefit?
- How will the city/state benefit?
- How will the country benefit?
- How will families benefit from this project?
- How will kids benefit from this project being successful?
- What will our work mean to future generations?

Sometimes it is helpful to contemplate these questions and re-connect with a greater sense of purpose. If able, invite others in the workplace to also explore these contemplations. You may be surprised.

Instead of just doing a job, you may find you can feel part of something worthwhile, something that provides benefit to many. And in facilitating this, you may find you will create a more aligned and harmonious workforce and avoid a few catastrophes along the way.

What Does Your Heart Want?

"What does your heart want?" might seem like an odd question, so hang in there for a moment. We live in a sometimes crazy world. How many people do you see who sacrifice their peace of mind and place themselves in financial peril, just so they can have a car they cannot afford, to be seen driving it.

In a quiet moment, I would ask you what you want in this world. Many people's answers would be wealth, a better job, an amazing house fully paid off, or even a better body. But how important are those things – really?

I look at my life, and I think about what I want. I want my kids to be happy and my grandchildren to be able to grow up in a peaceful world. I want them to live long lives and be free of accidents and disease. I want them to never have to go to war or experience trauma. When I look further, I want the world to be a safe place for all kids. I want you and your family to have the same safety and peace that I want for mine. I never want to see your sons or daughters go off to war.

If I lost one of my kids, you could not give me enough money, fame, houses, or cars to take away my grief and sadness.

But the terrible twist I see is that so many parents back in the city lose their sons or daughters to suicide because life has gone off the rails. To you, he may be a bloke who worked on this site, but he is some mother's little boy.

In our modern society, in our quest for wealth, attention, nice cars, cool houses and all manner of other "must-haves", we have forgotten what we really do want.

There is nothing wrong with having a nice house and a nice car, but there is a difference between needing it to make yourself feel successful and wanting it because you can afford it, and it would be nice to have.

The Economy of Things

When I was five years old and starting school, I did not really care much about other kids other than whether they wanted to play and go on some adventures. I had no attention on what their parents did for work or what sort of car they drove. None of that was important. These were my friends, and we played together.

Over time, I picked up on a few things. Television told me of people who were rich and famous and powerful. The idea of having a lot of money was appealing. Soon, I got to the place where I realised that I was one of the people who did not have money. In some way, the people who did have money were better than me. They had some things I did not have – money and power.

It did not bother me much because I was basically happy, but the belief was sitting there in the background, driving my viewpoint and choices. Make money. It will make you powerful and happy. I found myself wanting to find ways to make money, and so I joined a few of the network marketing companies, tried a few business ideas, but never really made it.

I was never without but just could not score the "big bucks". There was a point where I realised that focus was taking me away from creating what I really wanted.

The challenge is that our entire economy thrives on people doing everything they can to make money. For 60 years, our economy has been built on the belief that the economy must grow. Some people know how to work the system and make the cash. Others do not and must settle for a wage or salary. Then there are others who settle for the wage and patiently, over time, build their savings and slowly build wealth.

After the second world war, the primary focus in Australia was to build the economy. People were encouraged to spend. Demand drove production, which created more jobs, and the economy grew. It was a national goal. By the mid-'70s, we had done a good job of it, but no new goal was created, so the "grow the economy" plan rolled on, with no real goal or endpoint.

Companies got better at doing business, and marketers and advertisers got better at seducing. Hollywood chimed in, and soon we began to revere the wealthy. It has been such an amazing flow that saw the majority of us become lost in a competitive struggle to accumulate and prove ourselves successful.

And all the while, marriages fell apart, drugs infiltrated our society, and crime thrived. Some places became dangerous to live in.

We lost connection with the fundamental things that make us happy. Instead of seeking to help our friends, we battled to be a bit better than them.

And the amazing thing is that every brand-new car I bought, they were fun to have, but I realised they did not improve my life. It was still me, and I had a new car.

These situations and how we respond are our egos at work. I refer to a previous chapter where I talked about how our egos can get us into strife. Egos are not bad. They are just egos. But when they make a decision on our behalf that place us in an unstable position, it is time to get real and look at our life.

Egos create, but sometimes they get a bit out of control. As the Skyhooks sang, "If you have an ego, you gotta keep it in good shape". If it was not for someone's ego, we would probably not have an Opera House or a Harbor Bridge. Many of the mines around the country probably would not exist.

Our egos can get us into deep water sometimes, but if we fail to learn the lessons about deep water and about swimming, we will drown, or we will find ourselves in even deeper water.

So here we are in Australia, evaluating our life success by the things we can buy. Of course, there is nothing wrong with owning a beautiful house and a nice car and lots of toys. But if the debt you carry to support that is crippling you, and keeping you trapped, then you are crazy.

But without people borrowing money to buy things, the economic growth we have convinced ourselves we need would not be there. As soon as you have a well-paying job, people will be out to convince you to buy things. Having money in your pocket will facilitate you noticing advertisements for nice things too.

All of that is just temptation. It is designed to seduce your ego into making a purchase. Everything is lined up, including the finance, to make it easy for you.

But you do not have to play the game. You can stop for a moment and ask yourself, what do I really want in my life? What is important to me?

When the Head Rules

When we get lost in our ego, our mind, or our head, as I like to call it, begins to dominate. It will convince us of anything. We march off down a road of decision making that will ultimately lead us to harsh life lessons.

When we let our head runs things, we over-ride the fundamental things that make us happy and start to get caught up in the things that excite us. Our minds can seduce us with so many stories about why we should get that thing or why we need that thing. But it is just the mind. It knows nothing of happiness.

Read that again.

Our mind knows excitement, thrills, fun, adventure and risk. But it knows nothing of genuine happiness.

Our hearts know where happiness is. Our great challenge is to get out of our minds and feel what our hearts really want. When we truly understand this, then it takes courage to travel a path that honours what our heart really wants. We will need to stand strong against expectations and judgements from others. But here is the exciting thing. When others place an expectation on you or cast judgement, it is just their minds and not their hearts. So, it is ok. If you stick to your guns, one day, you will be their inspiration for getting their life back on track.

I love to hear stories about so many post World War II immigrants who came to Australia from countries like Greece, Italy, Yugoslavia, Hungary, Czechoslovakia and Poland. Many of them came and did labourers work or manned the machines in textiles factories. They turned their backyards into farms and lived frugally, spending time with family and friends, living a simple, village-like existence in a big city.

They saved their money, and as their savings mounted, they bought houses. Many of those families are among the biggest owners of residential real estate in Australia's major cities. They chose not to fritter their money away on luxuries but to build stability for their families.

You can do that too.

Your Inspiration

Bottom line – it rises from your heart, not your head. My advice to you is to get much more interested in the things you care deeply about. Perhaps it is the environment, or social justice, or kids being safe and given equal opportunity.

Perhaps for you, it is art, or theatre, music or photography. Perhaps it is growing food and cooking so you can bring people together around a table to connect and enjoy each other's company.

Perhaps your passion is building things or resurrecting things that are decaying, like an old car or a piece of furniture. I am scratching the surface there.

Whatever it is, in your role as a FIFO worker, you have the time, space and the income to support you to explore and discover. You are in a wonderful position to work out why you are here this lifetime.

If what I have written here touches you and you are keen to explore more deeply, get in touch. I may be able to point you in a helpful direction.

Chapter Summary

Why does the pre-Christmas wind down create so much stress?

If things are not as you would like, what would you prefer?

Without something worthwhile to do, we do not thrive.

What would you rather be doing with your life?

Perhaps we are all born with a spark of inspiration. For some it is obvious. For others, not so.

Have you ever contemplated your true inspiration for this life, your deepest sense of purpose?

Lack of purpose can equal boredom. Perhaps it is time to get interested, to start exploring.

Perhaps taking on a FIFO role gives you that time to really contemplate and explore why you are here on the planet. Whilst you are stowing away a bit of a financial nest egg, you might very well discover what it is you really do want to do this lifetime.

Sometimes it is our beliefs about security that limit us.

How will you feel about this life as you draw your final breaths in old age?

Calming the mental noise is crucial to allow contemplation. Meditation, long quiet walks, engaging in art or music or taking up a hobby can help to quiet your mind.

Worries about what other people think give you a clue as to the beliefs that might be holding you back.

Genuine life purpose always seems to be something that will benefit another person or people, in some way.

We should not need a catastrophe to help us get our eye on a worthwhile goal. We can choose our own goal.

What does your heart want?

Take a moment to fully feel the ripple effect of someone taking their own life.

In modern life, our quest for status, nice things and must haves, have taken precedence over what we really want.

We have belief structures about money wealth, success, power and how they all promise happiness.

Understanding the economy is a key to building what you desire.

What is Australia's goal other than to "keep growing the economy"?

Yet as the economy grew, many challenges came with it as society began to fall apart. Crime, violence, drugs, marriage breakdowns, homelessness all appeared.

Egos are important to our creative power, but when they get a little out of control, we can create unwanted challenges. Learning the lessons is crucial.

The thing that never changes is the age-old case of temptation. In the modern world, the temptation is to do what it takes to "have", even if it means borrowing and creating debt.

Head over heart, or heart over head. What do you really want as opposed to what do you think you need or "must have"?

Our mind knows excitement, thrills, fun, adventure and risk. But it knows nothing of genuine happiness.

It takes courage to travel a path that honours what our heart really wants.

We can learn lessons from the post 2nd world war migrants.

Finding your inspiration requires that you get more interested in the things you care deeply about.

Take time to explore.

Life Tips from This Chapter

Take time to go walking quietly. Allow your mind to wander over things. Contemplate the things that you were passionate about as a teenager. Just allow your mind and your feelings to wander.

What are the things you care about most?

"What is that thing you do, that whilst you are doing it, time seems to disappear?" Therese Rein.

What things in the world get you angry? Perhaps it is an environmental or humanitarian issue. Is there something you would like to do in that space.

Check out this Channel on YouTube.

https://www.youtube.com/c/TheOutcomeChannel/videos

Specifically, watch the following video by Tom Bilyeu.

"How To Find Your PASSION In Life In 2020 | Find Your True Purpose."

Boredom, Loneliness and Using Time

Boredom can destroy you. Many people in our modern world are bored beyond measure.

In this book, I have discussed the importance of finding your passion and of having goals extensively. These things keep your attention on where you want to go. They are a bit like a carrot on a stick that keeps you moving forward.

However, I understand that many of you who are reading this book are yet to find your passion or a sense of purpose. And you have not found a set of goals that excite you.

My question is this. Are you going to allow boredom to destroy you, or are you going to bring your life under your deliberate control and use your time in ways that nurture you and keep your mind and body in good shape?

This is a choice point in your life. Go with the flow, whatever the flow happens to be, or make a deliberate decision and create something of value.

Downtime in Camp

For most of you who are reading this and working FIFO, you are living in a Camp and cannot go anywhere. Apart from the Mess, The Gym, the Wet Mess, and a few other minor activities, you are not overloaded with options.

Perhaps though, that statement may not be true. How you use that time depends on your own capacity to be creative. You will have at least a couple of hours each day to use as you choose.

For those of you who are at home while your partner is away, you too will have at least a couple of hours per day that you can make use of or waste.

Each time I have stayed in a camp, I am always inspired by the number of people I see in the gym working out at 4:00 am in the morning. These are people who have decided to make the most of their time, with great facilities so close at hand and improve their physical fitness.

So, what can you do with your downtime?

A few beers

Whilst staying in camps, I notice two diverse groups of drinkers. First, there are the bigger groups in the Wet Mess, drinking plenty, getting loud and often stirring things up. It would be easy to drink a lot there.

Then there are the workers who like to gather in pairs, or small groups of 3 or 4, and have a few drinks outside someone's accommodation quarters (dongle).

The latter is probably a better choice as the conversation is more likely to be relaxed and non-competitive. It will be more about friendly connection and quiet discussion.

In big groups, you can find people competing for attention, and it does not take a lot for tension to build between individuals. A pecking order often exists in such groups, and being around them can have a negative impact on one's self-esteem.

I have a sense the problem arises when the "few beers" happens every day. If you are a person who wishes to improve your life, a few beers every day is probably a dead-end street in the journey of your life. You need something else to do.

Getting Enough Sleep

It is important to talk about sleep. Later in the book, in the chapter on self-care, I cover sleep in a lot more detail.

However, it is important to mention sleep at this point.

Many of you, whilst at work, are not getting enough sleep. You get caught up in post-work activities and fail to give your body the chance to get the nurturing sleep it needs. In the long run, this can be disastrous to your health.

Things that interfere with good sleep include:

- Too much extended socialising
- Social Media addictions
- Television
- Pornography
- Over-eating
- Stimulants like caffeine and drugs.

If your night-time activities are impacting your sleep, how long do you feel you can allow things to continue before you start creating problems for yourself?

What would happen to your life if great sleep became a "number one" priority?

Destructive Downtime Habits

I have just been talking about things you can get involved in that can have a detrimental effect on you. I also ask you to notice your workmates. Are they getting involved in things that are counter-productive to their growth and happiness?

Social Media

Since 2008, Social Media has come from nowhere to everywhere. Social Media companies have grown from being a fun idea into the world's largest corporations.

How did they do it? I feel that a big part of it was that they accidentally discovered a magic formula that relieved our collective boredom. But with it has come profound change, even to the point where we see young kids and teenagers taking their own lives simply because of what is happening online with their peer groups.

It is an amazing phenomenon. I listen to parents lamenting angrily about how addicted to social media their kids are, only to have them become distracted by an update on their phone. I know it well because I, too, was at the effect of it.

I had to reign in my notifications when I bought my first Apple watch because I was being distracted every few minutes by unimportant alerts.

Do you really need to be receiving notifications? If not, turn them off. They will still be there when you are ready to read them.

Second, when you post, are you fishing for responses or simply posting for the interest of anyone who might want to look? If you are fishing for responses, you will need to be creative and resilient. Sometimes you win, and sometimes you lose.

It can be helpful to have a "content creator's" mindset. Post things just to be of service to others. You find something funny or of interest, or you may even take a nice photograph. When you post, do it with the attitude of "perhaps someone will get some joy from this, or will find it helpful".

Using social media this way, you are seeking only to give and not to receive. Then, as you observe other people's content, you can leave encouraging notes where appropriate.

Dark Corridors

Recently I listened to a fabulous Joe Rogan Podcast with Tristan Harris (episode #1558), a former Google Employee. Harris was heavily involved in the production and presentation of the Netflix Documentary, The Social Network.

It was astounding. He shared in detail how the artificial intelligence (AI) machines work and how they track everything you do on Social Media and line content up for you.

They play a cleverly calculated prediction game as to what to feed you next.

If you are not very deliberate on Social Media, the AI will seduce you down all sorts of unhelpful paths. And remember, this AI has neither a heart nor a conscience.

Harris shared details of a famous case where young girls aged in their early teens who were viewing diet videos on YouTube were eventually fed a series of videos about anorexia nervosa. This is deeply disturbing. A huge outcry followed, and some modifications were made. However, the fundamental methodology remains unchanged.

This past year, there have been so many conspiracy theories running about what is happening in the world with the Covid-19 Pandemic. I have found that if I watch just one of those, more seem to find their way to me. So, I stopped watching any of them.

The warning signs are there. I have never worn any brand of running shoes other than New Balance since 1980. They are perfect for me. During the pandemic, I bought a couple of pairs and some running gear online. Now, wherever I go on the internet, I am greeted by wonderful advertisements for New Balance.

If you think someone is watching you, they are. It may not be a human being, but there is an intelligent presence tracking your every click.

I have been doing some reading, and it seems that you can throw the AI off by taking some time each week to view things you would never normally watch.

Gambling

I grew up in Pubs and was once shocked to learn that many of the regular patrons would rather go without their beer than miss out on a punt. That never really fitted through my window.

But perhaps it was true. In those days, to place a bet, you had to leave the pub or your home and walk to the closest TAB. Then you would return and listen to the race on the radio.

Some men often bet but in small amounts. It was a game to them. Others bet more heavily, sometimes had good wins, and often suffered big losses.

The difference back then was that it was difficult to hide. You had to make your way to the TAB and go inside. Everyone saw you. If you went to the racetrack, you were a little more anonymous, but still, people knew you had gone to the racetrack. It was harder to be a problem gambler and hide it.

Modern technology now allows you to gamble on so many different things and keep them completely hidden from the world. There is nothing external to you to help you control either a compulsion or an addiction, except, of course, the balance of your bank account.

I recall a regular event on "Pay Day", which was always Thursday. Women would come to the pub and meet their husbands as they walked in the door. They would take his pay packet, give him some drinking and betting money, and leave.

My parents were also responsible pub owners. If a bloke drank too much, they would either send him home or make sure someone took him home. If a bloke had a gambling problem, they would seek to help.

Who is looking out for you, or your mates, if you or they get caught up in gambling? Online Casinos and Sports Betting Apps have been the cause of many marriage breakups and the liquidation of countless family's assets.

The bottom line here is that any form of gambling is risky behaviour. You may think you have it under control. But do you really? It becomes a disastrously slippery slope when you begin seeking to win back what you have lost. It is a game that very few people can win.

I have a sense that for many, there are old impressions of masculinity, manhood associated with having a punt. Back when I was a kid, that is what men did. They drank beer and had a punt. But like many old impressions, some of those must die for us to evolve and get better at being good human beings living in modern society.

Life was simpler back then. There were different demands, fewer pressures, and life was a little slower. Everything was cash-based and much more in the open.

A Self-Assessment

I ask you to consider something. If you are going to either start gambling, or continue gambling, ask yourself the following questions and answer them to your partner, best friend, boss or one of your parents.

1. What is your intention for gambling? Why are you really doing it?
2. Do you have a weekly limit, and can you be absolutely certain you will never go over that limit?
3. Does your partner know that you are gambling, and do they know the fullest extent of your gambling?
4. Could you stop, right now, if your partner asked you to?
5. Do you ever regret your losses and find yourself thinking about them, wishing you had not lost?
6. Do you find yourself looking at Gambling Apps or Websites when you should be sleeping, or at times during the day when you should not be looking at your phone?

Now, score your responses:

For Q2, for Yes, score zero. For No, score 1 point.
For Q3, for Yes, score zero. For No, score 1 point.
For Q4, for Yes, score zero. For No, score 1 point.
For Q5, for Yes, score 1 point. For No, score zero.
For Q6, for Yes, score 1 point. For No, score zero.

What is your Total Score? If it is 1 or above, you have a gambling problem. If it is 2 or above, you have a severe gambling problem. If it is up at four or five, you need to tell someone and come clean. You need help.

Gambling Support Services

Victoria – Gambler's Help
Phone: 1800 858 858
Website: https://gamblershelp.com.au/

New South Wales
Phone: 1800 858 858
Website: https://www.gamblinghelponline.org.au/services-in-your-state/new-south-wales

Western Australia

Phone: 1800 858 858

Website: https://www.gamblinghelponline.org.au/services-in-your-state/western-australia

Queensland

Phone: 1800 858 858

Website: https://www.gamblinghelponline.org.au/services-in-your-state/queensland

South Australia

Phone: 1800 858 858

Website: https://www.gamblinghelponline.org.au/services-in-your-state/south-australia

Tasmania

Phone: 1800 858 858

Website: https://www.gamblinghelponline.org.au/services-in-your-state/tasmania

Northern Territory

Phone: 1800 858 858

Website: https://www.gamblinghelponline.org.au/services-in-your-state/northern-territory

Productive Downtime Activities

You can use your downtime for productive efforts.

I do understand that while out on site, you work hard. So, I am not suggesting you should do anything. That part is up to you. But if you can motivate yourself, you might surprise yourself. You might find something you can do for a few hours per week that will turn into something magnificent after a couple of years of sustained effort.

Study

You could enrol in a course. If you check out all the options available at Open Universities, you might find something that is appealing.

While at work, you can do as much as you can and then catch up during your time at home. There are so many things you can study. Here are a few:

- Cert 4 in Safety,
- Certificate in Workplace Wellness
- Nutrition
- Personal training
- Organic Gardening
- Website Development
- Property Investing
- Real Estate
- Counselling Certificate
- Wine Making
- Part-time Degree
- Sports Coaching
- Sports Club Administration
- Many others.

Learn a Language.

Have you thought about learning a new language? Perhaps you started a language at school but did not achieve proficiency. There are apps like Duolingo or Babbel and courses on YouTube.

Perhaps you can get a few mates together, or work with your partner, and do it together. For couples, this is a great activity to work on together whilst you are apart. You might even set a goal to visit the country where the language is native in a couple of years for a holiday.

Start a Fitness Quest

You could use this time to get your body back into shape. Most camps have a good gym, and some have a swimming pool. In addition, you can do Yoga anywhere.

Online you can find all sorts of Apps and Websites where you can follow programs. If you are truly serious about this, consult the activities coordinator onsite or consult a personal trainer at home and have them create a program for you. Stay connected to them and follow their advice.

If you are keen, you might throw out the challenge to a couple of your workmates and work with them to achieve your goals. Working with mates helps to keep everyone motivated and on track.

Take on a New Hobby.

Have you ever wanted to play a musical instrument or to become a writer? There are so many new skills you can build because you have time.

Perhaps you have wanted to learn to meditate, draw, or write poetry. You have wanted to learn how to edit videos. You have time. All you need to do is some initial research and then get started.

The cool part about this is that it does not matter how good you are or how good you get. The path you choose is your journey, and you are doing this to challenge yourself, learn, grow, and ease your mind.

I met a man some years ago who took up painting when he was 85. His skill developed, and he became quite a good painter.

Build a New Skill

Perhaps you have never been a good swimmer. If your camp has a pool, you might decide to work on your swimming until you can swim. Early 2020, when my son turned 30, I talked to him about his weight gain and his apparent loss of fitness. He had been super busy growing his business and had forgotten about caring for himself.

I asked him if he would like to train together, and he jumped at the idea. He is a big guy, 195cm and over 105kg, so I knew running would not be a good start. I also knew he was not a great swimmer. As a kid, his interest was music, and he had little interest in sport, so getting him engaged was a challenge.

I suggested we meet at the pool and spend some time working on his swimming. He liked the idea. We started mid-January, and he worked hard at it. He was a good student. By the time Melbourne's first lockdown came in March, some 89 weeks later, he swam 2.2km in a session. It did not take long.

Whatever you put your mind to, if you access the proper guidance, you can learn.

Do You Really Need that App?

Take your phone out for a second. Are there any apps on there that drag your attention, apps that you struggle to leave alone?

Are these Apps helping you achieve your goals and supporting you to become the person you want to be?

I use Apps. I am thankful for Cricket and Football Apps that give me the scores when I cannot tune into a game. But if I am somewhere that I need to be fully present, I put my phone away.

For example, when I am home with my partner, I put my phone in the bedroom. I do not need it then. When I meet a friend for coffee, I either put my phone in my bag or leave it in the car.

That is the phone. But what about the Apps. A few years ago, I found myself checking Facebook all the time. It was distracting me and taking my attention away from where it needed to be. It was a problem. So, I closed my account and left it closed for over three months. It was a good thing to do. When I re-opened it, my desire to check Facebook all the time was gone.

For some of you reading this, it might be a dating site consuming your attention, a game, share trading or another app. It is your responsibility to evaluate your situation. If you cannot control your use of the app, do you need to remove it for a while?

It is like a person trying to lose weight who chooses to carry chocolate bars around in their backpack. It is not healthy for your stability or your self-esteem to continue to expose yourself to powerful temptations.

I leave the decision with you. You can use this time for self-evaluation and genuine self-honesty. If you aim to create a better life, it is good to remove those things that may be opposed to your goal. When you do this and master your capacity to delay gratification, your self-esteem will improve. You will like who you are becoming.

Chapter Summary

Boredom can destroy you. Many people in our modern world are bored beyond measure.

Finding your passion keeps you moving forward.

How do you plan to use your time? For your good or your demise? A choice point: Go with the flow or create something of value.

In camp, there are not a tremendous amount of downtime visible options.

You have at least a couple of hours each day to use as you choose.

The same goes for the partner at home. You will have at least a couple of hours that you can use deliberately or waste.

In camp, you can get caught in the wet mess and drink a lot, or you can have a couple of quiet beers with mates away from the noise.

Big groups and alcohol do not usually go well together.

A few beers are ok, but perhaps not every day. Who is in control? You or the beers?

Sleep is crucial to your well-being. Conversely, sleep deprivation can be disastrous to your health.

Are your end of shift activities compromising your sleep or nurturing your sleep?

What are your mates doing in their downtime? Are their activities supporting them to get adequate sleep?

Social media came from nowhere to become a powerful force in modern existence.

Parents complain about their kid's screen time, only to have their complaints interrupted by the arrival of a text. It is ever-present in everyone's life. Good or bad!

Do you need your notifications turned on? The distraction can be catastrophic.

When you post, what is your intention? Are you seeking to share something helpful, or are you fishing for likes and responses? Are you honest with yourself?

Have a "Content Creator's" mindset. Post things for the benefit of others, entertaining or educational and do not be fussed if nobody appreciates it.

Seek to give, not receive.

Social Media AI (Artificial Intelligence) is designed to track and seduce you. But, unfortunately, this AI has no heart and no conscience.

Get smart and throw the AI off your trail. Instead, watch some knitting and gardening videos for a while.

Before the Internet and online gambling, it was harder to hide your gambling from loved ones and associates.

With online gambling, there is nothing external to help you control your compulsions and addictions.

Who is looking out for you or your mates if the gambling bug bites you and you get in too deep?

It becomes a disastrously slippery slope when you begin seeking to win back what you have lost.

Punting does not make you a man. On the contrary, it is more likely to make you a fool.

Did you take the Self-Assessment?

What can you do in your downtime?

Study – Certificate 3 or 4. Perhaps an Open University Course?
Learn a new Language. Get some mates involved and learn together.

Start a Fitness Quest. Set a goal.

Take on a new hobby. Research, learn and develop.

Build a new skill. It can be anything. Perhaps you will learn to play a musical instrument or to dance, or practise a style of yoga or martial art.

Evaluate your Apps on your phone. Which ones do you not need that tend to distract you? Then, either turn off notifications or delete the App.

Do you need Facebook on your phone? Or can it wait till you get to your laptop later?

"You must take personal responsibility. You cannot change the circumstances, the seasons, or the wind, but you can change yourself. That is something you have charge of." ~ Jim Rohn

Life Tips from This Chapter

Talk with your mates and set a workable limit on the number of beers you will drink.

Create a Sleep Routine and follow it. See the chapter later in this book related to sleep.

Download a Sleep App to help improve your sleep.

Make some deliberate decisions about Social media. Which apps do you need to be on, and which ones are just consuming your attention.

When you go to bed, turn your phone off.

If you have a gambling or porn habit, talk to someone about it. If you hide it, it will not go away.

Consider doing a course online.

Chat to your regular workmates and learn a language together.

Commence a Fitness Quest.

Find an online course to become a Personal trainer or Yoga Teacher.

Learn a musical instrument or commence acting classes.

Start a Fund raising program for a charity or cause you care about.

Take up a role for a local sports club that you can fulfill remotely. Every community sports club needs people who can help.

An Interesting thing about People

I sat and contemplated the rising rates of Mental Illness in Australia, seeking to understand why people living in such a vibrant and wealthy economy can find themselves feeling anxious, depressed, and stuck.

I asked myself what the difference is between people in these current generations and the people of my Grandparents' generations. How is their life different?

One could argue that when my Grandfather was around, people did not talk about mental health concerns, and people who felt anxious or depressed did not let on. And I could not dispute such an argument because I have no evidence.

But on the contrary, there does not appear to be much evidence to support that mental health concerns were as prevalent 100 years ago.

Life Has Changed.

How life has changed in the past 40 years. I was born in 1960, and personal computers did not appear till around 1983. I bought my first one in 1985, an IBM AT. It had a 20MB Hard Disk Drive, 512KB of Memory and cost me just $12,000 with a Dot Matrix Printer. The same year, a fully optioned Mitsubishi Colt Sports Pack cost me just over $10K.

I bought my first car phone in 1987, and my first mobile in 1990. "Smart Phones" did not appear till the iPhone arrived on June 29th, 2007.

And not a single science fiction writer predicted the Internet. I got my first email address in 1992, but it seemed like a waste of time because nobody else had an email. And if someone did email you a document, you could read it as it downloaded, line by line, because the download speed was so slow.

I remember once working on a grant application to Bell Atlantic, the giant US Telecommunications company. We were partnering with Carnegie Mellon University in Pittsburgh. At the time, we were developing ground-breaking game analysis systems for American Football.

As the Professor at Carnegie Mellon sent me the file, I had finished reading it before it was ready to save on my computer. I had my edits written in no time and could send it back.

Cars with computers in them did not exist 20 years ago. Likewise, video conferencing did not arrive till well after August 2003, when Skype appeared.

And look at the tools available now that make previously difficult jobs easy. For example, anyone with a "Bunnings Gift Card" and access to YouTube can make anything. But that is if it is not available already made at a lower price.

I watched a robotic system in a paint factory, packaging tins of paint. It stacked them on a pallet and then shrink-wrapped it. Not a human in sight!

In many American homes, kitchens have been replaced by microwave ovens. Many people now live on pre-packaged meals.

Building a Sense of Self

When reading my Grandfathers Memoirs, I was taken aback by a story he told.

Back in the 1920s, his father decided that diversifying the family business was prudent and the next major area of growth was beef cattle. The family owned Saltram Wines, in Angaston, and he wanted to build the family business.

He and his three sons loaded up their Model T Ford Tray Truck and drive from Angaston in the Barossa to Roma in the Darling Downs in Queensland. There, they eventually purchased three cattle stations with a collective boundary of some 170 kilometres. My Grandfather and his two brothers were to manage one each.

During one of their many trips between Angaston and Roma, the truck stopped out in the middle of nowhere. The engine still ran, but they had no forward momentum.

They pushed the truck off the road, waited for the sun to get low in the sky and then dug a hole about 5 feet deep. They wanted a hole deep enough to stand in so they could work under the truck.

The next morning, they got under the truck, took off the gearbox housing and discovered that a belt from the gearbox to the drive shaft had snapped. No belt, no forward motion.

One brother had an idea. So, they searched for a tree the right size, cut it down and then sawed off a disk of wood the correct diameter. They then proceeded to carefully cut away the bark and outer couple of millimetres of wood to create a new belt.

Once the new belt was in place, it got them moving again, and they made it to the next town.

The point of me telling you this story is that men of that era, people of that era, were faced with problems daily. They were forced to use their creativity and problem-solving skills to find solutions, and they were often required to perform back-breaking work to get the job done.

When they were done, there would have been an enormous sense of self-gratification from the success of their endeavour. This would have built self-esteem and a strong sense of self.

Every new challenge brought an opportunity for people to grow and to gain deeper levels of self-acceptance and self-esteem.

Where does that happen today?

The Modern World may have Neutered Many.

Many men, and women, gain deep satisfaction from their work. They are in positions where they are called upon to solve problems and bring solutions to life. Such people experience success in their lives, and they are likely to possess a healthy sense of who they are.

Every time I write an article, I feel good about it, I feel deeply satisfied, and I feel good about myself. The same happens when I have delivered a seminar that I feel has really connected some things for the people in the audience. It is deeply rewarding. I like who I am. I feel a strong sense of personal validity.

But what happens if you are in a job where your environment is tightly controlled and all you do each day is follow someone else's instructions and do what you are directed to do?

There is not much room for creativity in that.

When in your life do you get a chance to step up and use your problem-solving skills and your physical capacity for work to solve a problem or to make things better?

When we do something that makes life better for others or reduces suffering in some way, we gain an incredible feeling of personal satisfaction and validity. In those moments, our self-esteem grows.

If you do not experience those moments, and you have nothing to uplift you, then the reverse will happen. Your spirit may begin to die, and your mind may start telling you stories you do not really want to hear.

In a family situation or even in a community, many men (many people) relish the opportunity to help out and solve a problem. The challenge might be to fix a friend's car, change a flat tyre, or fix broken guttering on a roof.

The problem is that these opportunities are diminishing for a variety of reasons, including:

- Many cars cannot be started with battery cables anymore.
- People have become disconnected and do not like reaching out to neighbours. They would rather place an ad on Air Tasker.
- People spend little time outside their homes and so do not notice when help is needed.
- Many cannot afford a house, and so cannot make modifications that might improve their family's life.
- Due to the impact of modern life and the wealth of the average Australian, few people find they need a helping hand.

- About the only time where a person can show up and lend a hand and solve a problem or reduce suffering is during a crisis like a bushfire or a flood.

Many people travel through life with very few opportunities to serve selflessly, to do things that leave them feeling good about who they are. Life is too good in many ways.

There is a shortage of "traditional challenges" that give people the opportunity to grow.

There are Different Opportunities now.

Life has changed and the problems are different and much more subtle and harder to notice, but just as significant.

The problems that many people need help with are no longer in the "physical world", but exist in their minds, resulting from the choices they make, and the situations they create, in their lives.

People all around us are struggling with things like:

- Anger
- Aggressive behaviour
- Domestic Violence
- Alcohol abuse
- Gambling
- Relationship Difficulties
- Family Court conflicts
- Drug use
- Sick Family Members
- Debt problems
- Pornography Addictions
- Sexuality and Gender issues
- Conflicts with Teenage children
- Loss
- Many other things

Your tool in these cases is your care. It is expressed in your capacity to be interested, non-judgemental and ability to remain present and hold a space where a person feels safe to talk and express what they are feeling and experiencing.

In such cases, you may not be able to fix anything, but your care and presence will relieve suffering and bring hope. And when the time is right, you might be able to connect your friend or work colleague with the support they need.

This one may well be a slow fix. But your actions will help, and they will leave you feeling good about who you are. In the next chapter, I will talk about how to become better at noticing so that you can give care where it is needed.

"Where you are now is where you once decided you wanted to be. There is no sense in second-guessing the wisdom behind the decision. It made sense at the time." ~ Harry Palmer

Chapter Summary

There is a difference between our needs and our desires.

When our needs do not get met, our survival is threatened. When our desires are not met, our mind begins to react.

People from different times have similar needs but different desires.

We are constantly seeking to add convenience and make difficult tasks easy. But this is not always for the better.

The technology we have today is less than 30 yeas old, and now we struggle to live without it.

Overcoming challenges builds a stronger sense of self. When we take away all those challenges, we stop growing.

How do you thrive when living a daily life under someone else's direction?

Creativity is important. Do you get to use your creativity in your work, or in your life?

Do you get to do things in your life that make life better for other people?

Opportunities to help, on a physical level, are diminishing as technology and expanding service industries take the difficulties out of life.

There are different opportunities to help now. Many people need a strong and supportive guide to steer them away from destructive habits.

Care and Guardianship are your tools.

You may not fix anything, but you can relieve suffering and trauma.

We all need to build our skills in noticing what is going on around us.

Life Tips from This Chapter

Create a Book Club with friends or colleagues and choose some titles about life in the era of the first half of the 20th century.

Sit and talk with your Grand Parents if you can, or other elderly people. Find out what life was like for them. What was the hard stuff? What was the good stuff?

Perhaps try going camping somewhere that has no water taps, no toilets, no showers, and no telephone or internet signal. Get a sense of life away from all our modern comforts.

Spend a week eating foods that must be fully prepared. Bake your bread. Prepare all your vegetables and fruits. Perhaps even try hand churning some butter for your bread.

Try a Television and Internet free week. Learn what it takes to make an evening enjoyable when those two options are not available.

Practice Acceptance at the end of the day. Pick a thing that upset you during the day. It may have made you angry or frustrated, or worried or sad. Then write a list of 10 things that would have been much worse than that thing. Developing perspective helps build acceptance that things do not always go as you want them to.

Practice Gratitude for what you have. At the end of each day, write down at least ten things, from your day, that you are grateful for. Do this for a month and try to make the list different each day.

Learning to Care for Others?

Care is a thing we do not talk about much. I feel it is one of those things that has slipped quietly into the background as society became more focused on wealth and accumulation.

I do not think wealth and having nice things is bad. But somewhere, we got a little lost in the whole game of acquiring and perhaps became a little numb to what was going on around us. We can and should do a lot better.

The Changing Face of Care

Over time, I have watched with interest how the level of care in our society seems to have diminished. For example, in the '70s, older adults tended to live in their own homes till they died. Family members and neighbours would keep an eye on them and help out when needed.

Then sometime in the '80s, we saw a new model arrive where we could move our older citizens into residences to pay someone else to do the caring. I do not necessarily mean this to be a bad thing, just an interesting change.

Perhaps as a society in general, we became so busy that we no longer had time for our ageing parents, neighbours, and relatives.

Think Back 200 Years or more.

When settlers first arrived in Australia and spread out across this vast continent, they needed each other. So people worked together to build homes, clear fields and develop their communities.

Picture in your mind a half dozen cabins in the bush, some crop areas growing around them, a stream nearby, a vegetable patch and some animals. One person could not create that. Instead, it grew from a cooperative effort.

When storms came in, everyone worked together, making sure that everyone would be ok. Everyone had concern for everybody else's safety. Life was a little more vulnerable in those times, and everyone needed at least one extra set of eyes.

It was a natural tendency for people to look out for each other to ensure their safety.

Times Change

When was the last time you arrived home at night, pushed your key into your front door lock, and then stopped for a moment due to a worrying thought about one of your neighbours?

In our modern world, most people have a safe place to live, enough food and enough money to meet all their survival needs. Therefore, survival is not an issue for most of us, as I mentioned in a previous chapter. So, we have stopped keeping an eye out for what is going on.

But we all are aware that there is a mental illness epidemic right across western societies. People all around us are struggling with depression, anxiety, worry, insomnia and conflict. People are sad, angry, grief-stricken and lost in hopelessness.

It cannot be a genetic thing because if it were, then it would always have been there. However, there is a genuine identifiable link between gut health and depression. I will cover that in a later chapter.

What has happened, though, is less obvious and more common than most think. Mental issues start out with either bad decisions, messed up thinking, misunderstandings, not getting what we want, or committing transgressions that we knew were wrong, and at some level, we are in regret.

None of this indicates that a person is bad or wrong. It just means they have "gone off track" and, if their moral compass cannot get them back online, then they may need help. Unfortunately, however, in our society, we tend toward criticism and punishment.

Just about every religion refers to the errors in our judgements and how the wrongs we see in the world that leave us reactive are just reflections of the things we have done ourselves.

What would happen if we were more protective of each other? What would happen if we had enough awareness to notice when our friends make some odd decisions or go down a dangerous path? What would happen if we showed up for them right then? Would we be able to help them regain some common sense and see the errors in their thinking?

What would happen if you were onsite in the mess room and you walked past a young worker, and you noticed him opening a "sports betting" app on his smartphone? Would you just keep walking thinking he was an idiot? Or would you stop for a minute and get very interested in what he is doing? I am not asking you to make him wrong. Just get interested. You never know, he might have a deal with his partner that he has $30 play money each week to bet on the football, and she has access to it to monitor it.

On the other hand, that betting app could be his doorway to hell.

How will you feel eight years later when you find out he has lost the family home and can no longer see his kids because his betting habit was so out of control? I guarantee you would remember the moment you saw that app open on his phone.

The message I am giving you here is that we still must take care of each other. The dangers are always there. We are community beings who need to live in a supportive environment, sharing the good and the not so good of life.

My Friend Wayne

Back in 1980, I worked at The Golden Bowl in Camberwell, an eastern suburb of Melbourne. I was doing my third year of Physical Education studies and working this job to pay my bills and keep me alive.

One evening a bloke called Wayne walked in. He had just joined the gym and was looking to get into some training. He had recently completed his studies in Physiotherapy, was an A Grade Hockey player, a keen surfer, and a good bloke. I liked him immediately.

As we talked, I asked what area of Physio he wanted to explore. His reply shocked me a little when he said he wanted to break from it and explore something else. At the time, we were looking for another staff member, and I thought he would be perfect. So I raced out and told my boss, and he said, "Offer him the job!". That was recruitment 101 in 1980.

Wayne started working with us the next day, and we became life-long friends. But it was through my connection with Wayne that I learned some brutal lessons about friendship.

We were both transferred to work at a new club the owners had built. It was called The Ultimate Sporting Club and was Melbourne's first ultra, up-market health club. Everything was a pristine white.

We worked together for a couple of years, taking care of Politicians, TV Stars, Sports celebrities and Melbourne's upper-class elite. And most of Melbourne's leading models trained there, too, so I was always struggling to create coherent sentences when around them.

I left in mid-1982 to pursue my own path. Wayne stayed on for a couple of years till he found an investor and opened his own Health Club in Hawthorn. He did it differently and worked his butt off to make it a success. I used to drop in to see him often, and we would go for runs, talk about life and brainstorm ideas for improving his business. They were good days.

Eventually, we both met the girls we decided to Marry, and in July 1989, Wayne became a Dad. He was so happy and could not do enough as a Dad. Often, he would leave the house at 5:30 am to go and open the gym taking his baby son with him so his wife could sleep in. His business was doing well, and he was creating a lot of success.

It was a happy time. Six months later, my son was born, and we shared our stories. Then one day, a few weeks after my son was born, like a bolt out of the blue, Wayne's wife presented him with papers demanding a divorce. In the documents, she was seeking full custody of their son and 90% of the assets.

All of it was his before they met, so she wanted to take everything he had. There had been no animosity or conflict in the marriage. He was so profoundly shocked and bewildered by it. We went running on many occasions, and he talked it through. The following 18 months involved visits to courts, constant conflict and a lot of heartaches.

Eventually, the divorce proceedings arrived, and the perjury that took place in that courtroom would make your toes curl. His ex-wife won the case, took full custody of his son, and was awarded 90% of the assets. They painted him to be an abusive and neglectful father. He was never any of those things.

Of course, this is a familiar story where couples break up, and one tells lies to punish and defeat the other. It becomes more sinister when families decide that it is ok to endorse those lies instead of holding their loved one accountable for their bad behaviour. We can all learn from that.

We talked at length over the next few weeks, and I supported him in his grief. I asked what he would do, and he shared that all he could do was work. He said that he was about to pay out a ridiculous amount of money and that he may well lose his business. So, that is what he did for the next few years, working like a soldier to fill the pain of missing his son between his fortnightly catch-ups.

Here is my first miss. I remember thinking how angry he must feel. But I never raised it with him. I should have but left that to him. He never raised it, so we did not talk about it.

Over time, he got his business back on an even keel and started to get ahead. He was able to buy a unit near work and began to regain a reasonable lifestyle.

One day, when I dropped in for a run, he took me down to the car park to show me something. Sitting there in a prime parking spot was a beautiful Ferrari. When I asked whose it was, he told me it was his and that he had purchased it for picking up his son and drop him off at his ex-wife's place.

At that moment, I could feel the madness in what he had said. That was resentment gone crazy. Right then, I needed to take him, sit him down and not leave till he started to look at what he was doing and where he was going. But I did not do it. I had a lot going on in my life and chose to be selfish and turned it into a funny story that I told many times. So, I reckon I was 'in agreement' with his "payback" strategy.

Time passed. About four years later, I dropped in because I was going past. He said to me, "Just in time. We are going for lunch." When I asked where he was going, he told me that he was meeting some mates at The Clifton Hotel at Kew Junction.

I was a little gobsmacked and asked why he was going there. The Clifton Hotel at the time was a strip joint.

When I asked why he told me it was a heap of fun, the girls were amazing. I was pissed off at him. I told him I would never go into a place like that.

For the record, I am far from a prude. But I could not imagine what I would feel if I walked into a place like that and saw a friend's daughter on stage. It would be heartbreaking.

He told me I was a prude as I left, and I drove away angry. I was mad at him for stooping to that. But I was also angry at myself for having not dealt with this situation years before. It was clear that he was going off the rails, slowly but surely. I never did go back and sit him down and have that talk.

Some months later, I called to check-in, and he was in love. I had not felt him so happy for years. Unfortunately, the new love of his life was one of the strippers. He was in a new kind of struggle because her ex-boyfriend, apparently a standover man, was keeping her under a form of house arrest. This drama went on for months till one day the boyfriend disappeared without a trace. Wayne was united with his girl, and they spent their first 12 months together fending off questions from the Police about the whereabouts of her ex-boyfriend.

When I met her for the first time, the feeling was not nice. She was physically pretty, but I could feel there was a lot of darkness in her. Before the boyfriend who went missing, I learned later, her boyfriend was one of Melbourne's most notorious, slain underworld figures. She was bad news.

But it was too late to tell Wayne this. He was caught up in wild nightlife, wild sex and was having a good time. We still caught up, but not as often. I was travelling a lot for my work, and we both had our own lives. Eventually, he bought a farm on the Mornington Peninsula so that she could have horses. She had worked hard alongside him, and they had created success and some wealth. Everything was going great.

Then one day, when his son was about 20, he went down to the farm on a Friday, earlier than expected, and caught his girlfriend in the garage cooking up amphetamines. He reacted angrily and threw her out. That is when his troubles started.

He endured threats, harassment, letters from questionable lawyers demanding half of his assets for three years, and generally, he lived under a cloud of intimidation. In addition, she was utterly hooked on methamphetamine and had become wild and unstable.

Late November 2014, we caught up for coffee. He looked exhausted and stressed. I was perturbed for him, but he kept reassuring me that he would be ok and that it would all be over soon. As I drove away from the meeting, every cell in my body was on fire. I telephoned when I arrived back at my office but only got to his voicemail. Finally, I left a message to say I was worried about his welfare and wanted to know what I could do to help. Later that day, I received a return message telling me not to worry and that everything would be ok.

Ten days later, she and two other men kidnapped him, took him to a remote country location, and she taunted and tortured him for three hours before taking his life with a hunting knife. They threw his body down a ravine and then had sex on the grass under the stars.

He was missing for ten days before the Police found her and finally discovered what had transpired.

Eventually, I had to sit with his son, now 25, and look him in the eye and admit I had watched his Dad go off the rails for 25 years but had never done anything significant to help, to get him back on track. I apologised to him for that. He is a great young man. He looked at me and said, "Me too, John. I told myself Dad knew what he was doing, so I never said anything. I let him down too."

The girlfriend and her accomplices were charged and convicted of murder. And she has since been charged with the murder of her ex-boyfriend.

I tell you this story not to make myself bad or wrong. I tell you because the consequences of my dropping care for my friend were eventually catastrophic. When we notice things, we do need to act.

Many people end up in terrible situations in their lives. However, it does not just happen. It starts somewhere, and you never know when you might be the person who witnesses the "start point". When people are stressed, fearful, or even a little too full of themselves, they make some terrible decisions. These decisions can be life-ending.

Somebody always notices these moments, and they do have the chance to take action. And I am not saying you should know what to do. It is ok if you have no clue. But you can reach for support and share your concerns with people who have more confidence in such matters. Tag along, you will learn.

"A mistake is only an error. It becomes a mistake when you fail to correct it." – John Lennon.

Your Own Life

I want to offer you a few moments of contemplation. If you think back over your life, you will know and see times when you had an opportunity to step in and help someone but did not, and they ended up in strife. It is ok. You are a human being. We all fail, just like I did with Wayne.

I do not want you to make yourself wrong. That is a complete waste of time. But I invite you to avoid justifying your actions. When you do that, you learn nothing.

Just contemplate the events of the time. What happened, and where was it? What did you notice? What was the feeling you had that you chose to ignore? If you sit with it for a while, you will feel what it is. When you get to that place, you will learn what your mind did to over-ride what you felt, and you will learn something. If you do this well, you will not make the same mistake in the future.

All of us can get better. Unfortunately, none of us are perfect humans.

Helping Others

Sometimes events will happen that others will have noticed, but they did not act. Perhaps it is an accident at work, or something unpleasant happens at home or in the community. You can sit with those who were there and support them to feel what they felt and to notice the decisions they made and how they chose not to act. As you do this, from a place of interest and curiosity, you will help them to learn about themselves.

If you want to learn incredible skills for doing this type of thing, skills that would be a profound service in your workplace and your community, check in on the section at the end of the book on "Becoming a helper".

Strike When the Iron is Cold

I once learned something so unique that I have used it continuously for the past 25 years. When my son was 6, I was a single Dad, and I wanted to be a good and competent father. I knew I loved my son like no other person I had ever loved, but I knew my love would not be enough.

I was introduced to an incredible woman named Carolyn McLean, who ran parenting workshops in her home. She was amazing, at least 70 and almost blind, and her wisdom saved me. I went along weekly. I learned things that helped me be a better conditioning coach to the AFL players I was working with at that time.

One of the best things she taught me was "to strike when the iron is cold".

She went on. "Do not try to talk sense to your child when they are tired, stressed, hungry or emotional. It is a waste of time. Instead, wait till later, then sit down beside them and ask if you can have a chat about what happened earlier."

I tried it a few days later with my son, and it was incredible. He had zero resistance, and I learned what he was feeling and his frustrations. I got his side of it. We were both able to learn from what happened. Over time, we became much more able to resolve conflict.

But there is an important piece here. Do not try to sit down beside them when their attention is consumed by something else. You are interrupting them. I found the best time was to lay down with my son when he went to bed. We would read for a bit then have a chat. Those moments were gold.

You can do the same with workmates, friends, and members of your community.

Not Everyone Who is Behaving Like an Idiot is an Idiot

When I was 41, I was still running around playing Aussie Rules for a team in the small town in which I lived just outside Melbourne. I loved playing, and it was motivation to keep training hard.

One Saturday, we lined up against a team from a suburb situated in one of Melbourne's more "working class" areas. Many of these lads were covered in tattoos before tattoos became a more widely accepted art form. They were hard lads.

As the first quarter got going, one of their players, a big bloke, perhaps 6'1" and at least 100kg, a bodybuilder of sorts, with a mullet and lots of tattoos, was running around behind packs, king hitting my teammates.

I have seen that sort of thing before and have had to handle it. My usual mode of response would be to pick my time and put him to sleep. I was the biggest bloke in our team and certainly the most experienced. Having played VFA and having made it to All Australian Amateur level, I had come across some wild "lads". Some of them scared the shit out of me. But I stood my ground.

So here I was, getting ready to lay this man out "to protect my teammates". That was my justification, but I must have been growing up a little that day because as I ran around the ground, the realisation dawned on me that I was just as bad as he was.

The quarter time siren sounded, so as the two teams headed for their huddles, I ran over to him. Following is how the exchange went.

Me: "Hey Mate, have you got a sec? "

Him: (Taking a defensive stance) "What! "

Me: "It's ok mate, I just want to have a quick chat. "

Him: "What about? "

Me: "Well, you do not know me, but I am a pretty good bloke. All those blokes I play with over there – they are good blokes too. Some of them are Dads and their kids are here. And I imagine you are a good bloke too, and all your teammates. So, I am struggling to understand why you are doing what you are doing?"

In that moment, I thought his face was going to fall off."

Him: "Oh shit mate. I am so sorry. I can be such an idiot sometimes. I do not even think. I just get out of control. I am really sorry mate."

Me: "Ok, well I tell you what. How about you put your fists back in your pocket, let us have a really good game of footy and I will; buy you a beer after the game."

Him: "Yeah mate. Ok. Sorry mate. I am really sorry mate."

For the rest of the game, he ran around playing good football. Every time I took a mark, he would run past and say, "Good mark mate", and I heard him encourage a few of my teammates. At one point, whilst we waited for the ball to return to the middle after a goal, he ran into the centre square, put his hand on the umpire's shoulder and said, "You are doing a great job today umpy". He was a completely different human being.

After the game, he walked up to me in the social rooms and handed me a beer. I reminded him that the agreement was for me to buy him a beer. He told me that he owed me because he had not enjoyed a game of footy like that since he was a kid.

I was amazed by that. I said that I thought he had played a good game and rattled off examples of some of his efforts. I had attention on him during the game, so I noticed his achievements. He was chuffed. Then I said to him:

Me: "So what about that other stuff? How is that working for you in your life?"

Him: "Not very good?"

Me: "Have you got kids?"

Him: "Yes I do."

Me: "Do you see them?"

Him: "No I do not."

I tell you now, that is heart breaking. A fundamentally good man who cannot control his temper. I thought in that moment. "What have his football club been doing? Who is helping him?"

Me: "Do you want some help with that stuff?"

Him: "I probably need it hey."

Me: "Yes you do. I have a good friend who specialises in working with blokes just like you. Would you like to meet him?"

Him: "I guess I should hey."

Me: "I think so. What is your phone number?"

He gave me his number and I put it in my phone. We finally introduced ourselves.

Me: "Can I call you Monday morning"

Him: "Yes you can?"

Me: "What time suits best?"

Him: "10:00am."

Me: "So if I call you with my mate on the line at 10:00am Monday, will you pick up the phone?"

Him: "Yes I will."

The next day I called my mate and told him all about it. On Monday, I called my mate again and pulled the other fellow in on a three-way call and introduced them. We chatted for a while, and they aligned a time to talk, and I left them to it.

Sometime later, perhaps a year or so, I received a text from my mate telling me that he saw his kids that weekend. It was a wonderful text to receive.

I could have knocked him out and felt very self-righteous about it. But imagine the violence that could have erupted on that football field after that. That day, something healed inside me. And I was able to help heal someone else and give some kids their Dad back.

A Special Man

Back in 1994, I was CEO of a Computer Software company. We developed software and were the biggest supplier of IT systems to the fitness and Recreation industries in Australasia. We had great products.

A few years before, I was delivering a lecture in a Fitness Leadership Course, and a man in the course asked if he could come and visit me at work and see what I did. When he came in, he was fascinated. He came back to me with a proposal that he use a Centrelink grant to help pay his wage, and he would come to work with me and streamline all my operations. And the challenge he set himself was to create a full-time role for him. Less than two years later, I appointed him General Manager.

By 1994, we were also investing heavily in the USA and leading the race to produce high-quality non-linear editing systems for the NFL, the first computer hard-drive-based video editing system. We were way ahead of the game, but it was putting us under enormous financial pressure. I was travelling a lot, both interstate and back and forth to the US.

At the time, my son was four years old, and my wife was suffering extreme OOCD and addiction. I had so many balls in the air that I was struggling to remain present and effective. I was dropping responsibility and starting to justify and lie to cover my arse. I was out of control.

One day Peter asked me if we could have a chat. He said he was concerned and wanted to help me, and with a calm and gentle presence, he gave me all of it, right between the eyes. It was confronting and challenging, but I could not argue. He was dead right. I contemplated everything he said for a few days and began to clean my life up. It was hard, but I soon left my marriage. I could no longer assist my wife. She was refusing to take any responsibility and help herself. I had to get my son out of there because it was affecting him. I had to stop trying to rescue her and allow her to stand on her own two feet.

Peter did save my life that day. It was so courageous of him, but he did it from care. He knew who I really was, but at that time I had drifted off and forgotten who I was. Peter gave me a profound gift.

Selfishness and Care
Here is the brutal bottom line. Take a breath!

Ok, you cannot care for others if all your attention is on yourself. Selfish people are always worried about what they get, what they are owed and who has wronged them. So they talk about themselves, judge others harshly, and are never genuinely present to the needs of others.

What transpired in Melbourne during the harsh Covid-19 lockdown of 2020 was quite remarkable. The lockdown was challenging for many. Everyone was asked to wear a mask whenever outdoors. A tiny percentage of the population rebelled, but most citizens agreed with the measures and complied for the greater good.

Selfishness was set aside, and everyone did their bit. At the time, daily infections were rising rapidly, and Melbourne was headed to the same place as many international cities. Remember, Melbourne is a city of 5 million people that winter approached.

Slowly the numbers came down. People criticised, and the media painted a picture that life in Melbourne was akin to a concentration camp. But good-hearted Melbournians kept wearing their masks and stuck to the guidelines. Then, finally, the virus was eradicated. The genie was put back n the bottle.

Compare that to many American cities where people shout civil liberties and 2nd Amendment Rights and refuse to align. As a result, their infection rates went out of control.

Forgetting our selfish interests and placing our attention on the greater good allows us to be a contributor. As a result, we get to be part of the goodness of a community.

If you struggle with selfishness, think for a moment about all the kids connected with your site. Do you want any of them to suffer the devastation of a lost parent? Find within you that part of you that does care. It is there.

And sometimes it is good to tease yourself for being selfish too. That can help you to become more aware of it. Then, when you do handle it, I promise you will like yourself a lot more.

Listening so that Others Will Speak

When you approach someone to talk about their challenges, or about the things you notice, there are a couple of tips that can help. Remember, you are a friend, not a therapist. If you feel that your friend needs professional support, then it is good to suggest it and stick with them till they step into the care of someone who is trained.

When approaching someone, it is good to be beside them, not face to face. It is less confronting. I often ask a person if they would like to go for a walk.

People will often work things out for themselves. Let them know what you noticed. Do so without making it wrong. "I noticed the other day you said XYZ about your partner. I am curious about that. Is everything ok?"

Ask questions with interest. You are not interrogating. You are hopefully making it safe for the person to open up and speak more candidly about what they are experiencing.

Avoid giving advice. Allow the person to arrive at their own conclusions and have their own realisations. If you feel they are seeking a shortcut out of the conversation, just stay curious and compassionate. Keep asking questions.

If you need to give advice, ask permission first.

And always, at the end, thank the person for sharing with you. Ask if they need some support, and if so, help them to organise it. Stay with them.

If you feel it is important, you should ask the person if they mind you letting your manager know, or a person in management whom they feel comfortable with.

Check in on people from time to time after you have had these connections.

Chapter Summary:

Care is not a thing of the past. It was common in days gone by when physical survival was a real issue, but it is far from gone.

Times change. Abandoning the past is not always wise. New challenges arise, and in our times, the challenges come in the form of destructive temptations, secretive behaviours and bad decisions that can lead to stress, distress and mental ill health.

My story about my friend Wayne demonstrates how crucial it is to act and to show up for our friends, to help them before they slide too far.

Take time to contemplate the times you have dropped an opportunity to care in your life. Learn from it. What were the decisions you made that allowed you to over-ride what you felt?

Helping others is one of the keys to happiness. When we do good for another person and our actions really do help, then we end up feeling good about ourselves. One cannot help another without truly helping themself.

Strike when the iron is cold. It is a waste of time trying to have a meaningful discussion with someone when they are tired, stressed, hungry, intoxicated or distracted.

Not everyone who is behaving like an idiot is actually an idiot. If you judge someone that way, then you may well be denying a chance to help someone who is very much in need.

Get good mentors in your life. Speak to people you trust and invite them to be brutally honest with you from time to time. Develop yourself so that you can be that person for someone else eventually.

Selfishness is most often the enemy of care. It is important to take care of ourselves, but our greatest responsibility is the collective care of those around us.

Learn to be a good listener. Learn the skills of connecting with another person and communicating with them with curiosity, interest, and compassion.

Always help a person to get additional help if they need it.

Note: When you do get better at caring for others, you will like yourself more and will be less likely to engage in habits that erode your health and wellbeing.

Life Tips from this Chapter:

When you go onto a worksite, it is crucial that you have your awareness primed. This means having your attention out in the world, not locked up and ruminating on some repetitive set of stressful or angry thoughts.

Remember you are a human being. You will make mistakes, but your growth depends on you learning from those mistakes.

In Aboriginal Law, and many other forms of Indigenous Law around the world, once you have completed your punishment, or have made good for your transgressions, your slate is clean. What happened is gone. In our Law, we are not that forgiving. But in our personal and worksite relationships, we can be.

The Lakota Sioux Indians had a saying, "You are who you are. You are not what you have done." Keep getting better at becoming who you really are.

If you have worries, get them off your chest. Do not drag them around with you. You cannot be present when worried.

Create a connection with another person you trust and develop an agreement with them that allows you to tell them whatever you need to share, without being judged. Perhaps a local religious minister could be a good choice.

When you arrive at work and you feel a bit lost in your mind, a bit self-absorbed, do a meditation for 10 minutes to calm your mind and get your attention out into the world. See the Meditation Chapter at the end of this book.

Make a list of people you feel may be vulnerable and need some support from time to time. Check in with one of them every couple of days.

Do you have a hobby at which you are skilful? Are there any teenagers you know of who are struggling in life and may be uplifted by being introduced to your hobby?

Are there any older people you know who live alone and do not get many visitors? Could you visit them and find out what they like to do? Maybe you can include them in some community activities, like local sports clubs, so they can be around people, and perhaps even get to contribute.

Perhaps you can volunteer at a Soup Kitchen or a charity food distribution centre. There is a lot of work needed in packing food hampers.

Creating Safe Spaces for Others

We all need to take care of each other. Hillary Clinton, in her Presidential Campaign in 2016, borrowed an African proverb. "It takes a village to raise a child."

I believe this. I know from personal experience that not all fathers can be everything to their sons. While I am a complete jock, fully into sport, training, nutrition and everything that goes with it, I am tone-deaf, cannot draw even well enough to get invited to play Pictionary, and have no interest in cars.

My son, who I love so much, was never interested in sport, apart from a bit of tennis. However, he is musically and artistically gifted, loves gaming and is mad about his cars. Go figure right!

So, there were times he needed other mentors, people who "got" him. His maternal Grandfather was great for him, and I watch him today and see his Grandad's ways shining through.

Along the way, I have been able to fill a need for a friend's child or friends of my children. That is how kids make it, travelling their own path, finding the right mentors and guides as they go.

Community Clubs, Societies and Groups

One of the great beauties of local clubs like Football, Cricket, Netball, Hockey among a variety of other sports, Scouts and Guides, Art and Music Groups, Theatre, and others, is that kids can come together to share what they love, guided by parents who share that love.

In these settings, parents get to care for the kids, guide them and help them develop their passions.

But it is also a setting where parents can help other parents.

Once I took my daughter to Pony Club. I was shocked by what I experienced. Through my Physical education training, we talked about "The Ugly Parent", those parents who stand on the sidelines at sports games and abuse. We know them well, and much good work has been done to reduce this behaviour.

But, never before had I seen parents so openly abuse their children in front of others, as I did at Pony Club. Some of those mothers were so personally invested in how their children looked and performed that they became out of control, verbally abusive and even physically violent if the child was failing.

I stood in horror as I watched a mother screaming at her terrified child, forcing her to get back onto the horse she had just fallen from. All the other mothers looked away. So, I went to one of the organisers nearby and asked, "Who is going to go and help that woman and her poor child? Surely you are not going to turn a blind eye to that sort of behaviour."

She told me it was none of her business and that I should just let it be. My daughter was horrified that I might make a scene, so I backed down and then raised it with some women I knew in the school community who were part of that club. I assured them that I felt they needed to address it; otherwise, someone like me might contact the Department of Health and Community Services. I did not want to be threatening them, but I did wish to encourage them to take some action.

If I see a man at an Under 14 football game angrily abusing a 16-year-old umpire, I must ask myself this. If he is ok doing that here, in broad daylight for all the world to see, what is he doing at home when the doors are closed? In such a case, I would go and have a chat with him and help him. I am not saying you should do the same, but you can go to Club officials and ask that they do something and hold them to it. That man needs help. And his family may need help too.

These are the most powerful moments where we can create a beneficial ripple that flows through the community.

Domestic Violence in Your Community
In these modern times, domestic violence is a scourge that continues under a cloak of silence. Occasionally we read terrible stories of the final act of a man inflicting the ultimate harm on his estranged wife and perhaps his family. First, we feel horror, and then, not knowing what to do, we return to life and feel impotent.

Learning the Lessons in Domestic Violence

I recently read a powerful article penned by Dr Karen Williams and published on the ABC News Site, February 2020, titled "When men were being killed on the street, we took action. So why is domestic violence different?", by Karen Williams. The article outlined an argument that things seem to happen when it comes to men, but not so for women.

The article is very beautifully written and raises some sobering points. However, I will not recreate that here, as it is not the intention of this chapter.

When the "Coward Punch" issue became headline news, I contemplated the problem for some time. Finally, I concluded that if we are to stop the coward's punch and all other forms of reactive violence, I must first handle my own surges of anger that sometimes arise when things are not as I would like.

Handling My Own Anger

How do We Stop the Tragedy of the Coward's Punch?

For those of you in Australia, or for those who have seen it on YouTube, the campaign headlined by Champion Boxer Danny Green and several other notable men was blunt and in-your-face.

The advertisement is graphic, intense, and hard-hitting, but I wonder if it did as much good as hoped to change things. I genuinely hope it did, but perhaps it will not simply be as easy as that.

For years, we have been showing graphic and confronting advertisements depicting the harsh realities of irresponsible driving by young drivers. Has that stopped the carnage? Perhaps. Perhaps not. We continue to read about horrendous accidents where young people lose their lives whilst speeding or driving dangerously, seeking thrills and pushing their limits.

The Coward Punch we speak of involves one person coming up to another, generally from the side or behind, and punching them hard and violently to the head. The victim, without warning, is struck by a vicious and violent blow. In many cases, this results in death. In others, it results in brain damage and, in the rest, at least some form of injury.

The psychological wounds can be profound and enduring. The impact on families can be devastating.

So why do people do this? What makes a person simply abandon all common sense and become so overwhelmed with rage or payback that they can walk up to an unsuspecting victim and bash them so violently.

Well, I suppose a good place to start is in my own universe. I have done it. I remember when I was 15 and playing football. With a bad attitude and a taste for violence, a guy on the opposition hit two of my mates. Both were taken from the field, bloodied and stunned. I was so overcome with rage that I decided to take the law into my own hands. About 10 minutes later, the player jogged past me, and I let loose with what could best be described as a "haymaker" and punched him as hard as I could in the face.

The whole ground stopped in dead silence. Until then, my nickname had been "The Gentle Giant", as I was already 6' 4" tall when I was 15 and a pretty docile kid. Nobody could believe I had done it. But in my mind, I had stood up for my mates, and I loved the feeling of power it gave me.

Soon, I was belting blokes who dared even insult one of my mates. And I only ever did it on the football field. Why? I was a chicken and too scared to do something like that in real life. Fights on a football field are always going to be stopped. And I knew that.

But this act made me feel powerful, so I took this brand of intimidation into senior football. I was shocked years later when I bumped into an old opponent with whom I had many great tussles. There is no doubt he was a better player than me, but I used my size, strength, and threats to intimidate and dominate him. He said to me, "I hated playing against you. I was terrified of you". From my current perspective, that was a lot to feel and a most uncomfortable moment.

But see, this part of me still exists at some level today. If I see something terrible, some perpetrator or group of perpetrators doing something violent to a defenceless being, this part of my mind wakes up and the fantasy to bash rises like an unwanted tide. I feel the anger and hatred right there. Over the years, I have worked to integrate these areas of my consciousness, but the work is not yet complete.

So, my question to you, the reader. "Do you also have these bursts of rage when things happen in life? What do you do with it? What are you planning to do with it?"

See, I may not act on mine and may not have acted on it for over 30 years, but the fact it still exists means that I have a capacity for violence. That makes me a little better than the young guy who carries out the assault.

I feel that unless, as a collective society, we are all prepared to do the work on ourselves to become more enlightened and more peaceful, we are going to struggle to expect that our youth will comply. After all, where do they learn that rage in the first place?

I feel that unless we, collectively, are prepared to turn our anger and violent reactions around and become more compassionate, our lives will be regularly interrupted by the sad news of another innocent person dying senselessly.

Perhaps we can take this further, and I do so at the risk of offending some. How can we genuinely move away from these actions when our military use the same actions on people we do not like overseas. We are still so quick, as a country, to agree to go to war and unleash holy terror on the bad guys.

I know these things are complex and challenging, but what would happen if countries like Australia, the USA, and all the other developed countries in the world said, "That's it. No more war. No more bombs. No more treating violence with violence."

What would the world be like? Do you dare to dream of a brighter future? I feel we must.

Then if things ever do become tenuous between our country and another, we can challenge them to talks, a pie fight perhaps, and a feast to celebrate new agreements. After all, feasting has always been more pleasurable than fighting.

Back to Karen William's article

Referring to the Government's response to the coward punch situation and apparent inaction on domestic violence, Dr Williams argues, "So why is it, when we know of these patterns, do we not see a response from the legal system that reflects that understanding?

I would argue that when women have been brutally attacked in public, the public and Government response has been as significant as that related to the Coward Punch situation.

Domestic violence is a terrible thing. Yet, so often, it goes on behind closed doors and, due to embarrassment and socially driven fears, remains a secret. But it probably only remains a secret to those who ignore the things they notice.

I can go with so many directions on this topic, but I will hold to the one I feel requires the most exploration.

"The only thing necessary for the triumph of evil is for good men to do nothing."

~ Edmund Burke

We live in communities, and what goes on in our community can be accepted as a general reflection of the individual members' minds. Therefore, what we tolerate within ourselves, we will accept in our communities.

As I stated in my Cowards Punch article, I must take responsibility for my reactions, anger, and occasional internal surges of rage. I must own them as mine and not blame circumstances or other people for their existence. They arise in my personal universe. They do not come from another person or event but from how I view that person or event.

As I become more aware of myself and how I view the world, I am more present, deeply calm, and very aware. It is an excellent place to live, but the work is ongoing. There is no "perfect state".

Similarly, when I notice something that is not right around me, I have to handle it, or at least help. If it turned up in my universe, and it did if I noticed it, then it is mine to deal with. Hence my exploration of the behaviour of others around me. Do I ignore it, or do I help them with it?

And I do mean help because I do not like the "right-wrong" game. It does not help anything evolve. If I am at a football game and I see a supporter being abusive to a young umpire, I can ignore it or notice what is really happening. I can see a person with anger problems, and I do not need to be Dr Phil to know that anger probably plays out elsewhere. So, I need to help that person, care for them and those in their lives. It is the right thing to do.

If you are in that situation, you may not feel confident, but you can go and marshal other capable people and wake them up to their community responsibilities. But, again, I am not suggesting you put yourself in danger.

When Rowan Baxter was getting lost in his rage, and when the Domestic Violence Order was issued, where were his friends? Where were his mates? Did they not have a clue that this man was losing control? Where was the agreement between friends to track him constantly and keep him away from his family, to keep supporting him to talk through his rage and anger? Why was he ever left alone?

We can wait for the Government all we like, and we can blame them too. But the reality is that we do not have the spare police to give one-on-one care to potentially violent offenders. Locking them up might be an answer, but does it cure a problem or delay it?

The shoe must fit on both feet too.

I have had several friends who have been through the family court system and lost custody of their kids. These were good men, fathers who loved their kids and participated and engaged daily. But, in court, the lies that the wife and her family told were gobsmacking, all under oath.

I had another friend whose wife had a significant problem with alcohol and prescription drugs. One evening she went on a violent rampage, punching and kicking him. To regain some control of the situation, he grabbed her by the forearms and held firm till she calmed down. The next day she had faint bruises and charged him with assault.

Where were the friends and families of these women? Do they fail to support them, to be honest, respectful, and to refrain from using deceit to get their way or hurt their spouse?

Once I was walking with my partner, we overheard a terrible fight raging in our neighbours' home. We heard the wife yell, "You think you are so smart, but if you push me, I'll take the kids, and you will never see them".

My partner was horrified, and I said, "Well, it's your gig. You heard it. So, it's your job to help her with that." So, I agreed to catch up with him and have a chat too.

Abuse occurs in so many ways. Physical abuse ends up in injury, death, and horror.

Safe communities are places where citizens are prepared to have some guardianship and act on what they notice. The ablest citizens are the ones who have guardianship over their own minds, their reactions, and their emotions. There is never a valid reason for losing control – unless, of course, it is a moment of extreme danger where fear can overcome a person.

In this current economic climate of wealth and abundance, it is easy to get lost in the world of "me". We get caught up in what we want, what we should not be compelled to do, our social media status and how other people see us.

If we reflect on the times of the pioneers, they had no time to be concerned about any of those things because fundamental survival issues occupied their time and attention for the whole of each day. Survival issues dragged their attention out onto what was going on around them.

In our world of almost obscene comfort, that is not the case. So, part of our human challenge is to learn how to take our attention off our own selfishness and place it on the welfare of our community and our environment. That is the challenge that faces us all.

If more of us did the work to become much more aware, we would be there to help long before a person like Rowan Baxter becomes a figure of cruel and heartless terror.

Perhaps that is our life mission. Some might refer to it as a spiritual journey. But are you up for it? Are you up for stepping up and doing what it takes to extract yourself from your mind and become an aware and available citizen who can stand guardian and be ready when needed to care for a person or situation in need?

I think it is the most critical task in life, but it cannot be done by simply saying to yourself, "Right, I will be more aware now!". Instead, within hours, you will be checking your Facebook status to see if others think you are more aware.

It takes a commitment to personal growth to become a better human being.

What is Happening Next Door?
The following is an article I wrote during the pandemic in 2020.

I do not wish to date this book, but as I sit here in 2020, I realise that we live in genuinely fascinating times. But, unfortunately, none of us has a guidebook for this as almost nobody has lived through anything like it.

World Wars have a prominent and visible threat that brings people together. But, on the other hand, pandemics present an invisible threat that we cannot fight with a gun or hide in a bunker.

Unfortunately, what comes with such a threat is fear. In wartime, I imagine that this fear saw people become courageous and resolute, working together to oppose some form of perceived evil. However, it seems that during a pandemic, this fear turns into self-preservation, distrust, conflict, and abuse. Everyone else is a potential carrier of a virus, so they are all possible enemies.

My 63-year-old sister, who is slowly and very courageously working her way through stroke recovery, was appalled last week to see two elderly ladies brawling in a supermarket over a packet of toilet tissue. These women were probably some child's kind and loving grandma.

Last night I was a little stunned to read an email from an old friend. She cited a dictatorial government that people should stand up to as they take away our rights and freedom. She wanted to go about life as usual and ignore the pandemic. She felt that it was her right. But of course, that then meant in her eyes that the Government are wrong.

I wondered for a moment where someone with no training at all in the human sciences received all her incredible knowledge of pandemics. But alas, I could not help from that perspective.

The reality we face is that we all have minds. Minds tend to be mostly full of trash, and they can talk to us and tell us things. If we listen too much, we can go mad. I have experienced it personally. When playing football years ago, I remember being in many brawls; often, I was close to the flashpoint. In the wisdom of age, I realise now that a kind word at the time might well have been more helpful. Perhaps I loved the violence and heroics too much, along with the attention that comes with being a tough guy.

I have a sense it would be helpful for us to all realise right now that our minds are just minds, and minds are prone to madness. If we lose focus and shut down the wise guidance of our hearts, then we become little more than a person living on the edge of reactive savagery.

In times like this, living in communities, we need good people to step up and take notice, help others by using their awareness and good character to become more of a social conscience and take on a guardianship role in the community. Some vulnerable people need to be cared for and protected.

Further, domestic violence is an issue we all need to pay attention to in times like this. It is not a case of us thinking that people should not be violent. Some people are. We can debate the reasons or accept it because vulnerable people are at risk of abuse.

When the abuser is home more, and the effects of fear take their toll, we may be at risk of witnessing an increase in this terrible social scourge.

So, I have decided to keep my antennae up. I will stay alert to what is happening around me and make sure I notice when someone needs care and protection.

I do not suggest that you go alone to take on a violent and enraged offender. That is why we have police. But you can let the offender know they have been heard and that police are on their way.

And I leave you with something to consider. Our prisons are filled with people who made a terrible decision on a snap of reactivity. Their lives are ruined because they exploded and hurt someone. Many of these are fundamentally good people who lost self-control.

When you step in to prevent or interrupt domestic violence, you are caring for the perpetrator as much as you are the victim(s). Condemning someone who has lost control of their mind does not help. With this compassionate perspective, if you do know of people in your neighbourhood who tend to be reactive and violent, perhaps it is a good idea from time to time to take a mate and go check in with them to make sure they are ok and coping.

Domestic violence is a problem that will not fix itself.

In the Workplace

When I present to groups of workers in heavy industry workplaces, like construction sites and mines, I speak about taking care of what they notice around them to make the workplace much safer. This means taking notice of everything: from broken equipment to how a workmate talks about their spouse.

At work, we connect with many people, and we have the potential to notice many things.

Awareness is a funny thing. I learned a lot working in the AFL in high-performance roles. I noticed that when a player was having a bad day, his attention seemed to be more on himself. It can happen to anyone. Perhaps the player was fearful of a bad performance, or something might be going on in his personal life. At those times, the player gets stuck in his mind and extracts himself from the game's flow. It is incredible to watch.

Brendan McCartney, former Bulldogs Coach and Assistant at Geelong, Essendon and Melbourne, was the Seconds Coach at Richmond when I was a Conditioning Coach there in the late '90s. I remember him saying to the players, "I don't mind you having a bad day, but I won't tolerate you having a shit day".

He told them that you can still chase, tackle, shepherd, and smother, even when the ball might not bounce your way and give you an opportunity. But when a player has all his attention on himself, he does not even see the possibilities for the shepherds and smothers, and he certainly misses noticing his opponent moving away into space.

When at work, we can either have all our attention on ourselves, ruminating over how the world does not care, or how the boss is "an asshole", or fretting about missing a key event at your child's school. Or we can direct our attention out into the world to observe what's happening for the benefit of others.

When we are on a potentially dangerous worksite, every person has a unique perspective of what is happening, simply because of where they are standing or sitting. As a result, there are many sets of eyes, looking in many different directions from a multitude of standpoints.

But what happens if one team member is lost in their own thinking, all attention on self and none out in the world. That person may miss the very thing that needs to be noticed.

So, I ask you, when you are at work, do you have all your attention on yourself, or is it out in the world, taking an interest in what is going on. It is a good and helpful skill to develop.

There is another aspect to this too. I believe it to be vitally important. As you move about your site, and it may even be in the lunchroom, you will see or hear things that capture your attention for a moment. They may have nothing to do with the physical nature of your worksite but everything to do with the wellbeing of a work colleague.

For example, you may hear a colleague speak in a demeaning and derogatory way about their partner, perhaps to get a laugh. But, hearing it, you may feel that it is a really "off" comment.

It is when you get those feelings that you should act.

That person needs help with how they are behaving toward their partner. They need help to develop more reverence and respect. What they are doing is unkind and, at some level, it is cruel and abusive.

On another occasion, you may walk past a young worker and notice him opening a betting App on his smartphone. Innocent enough, I guess, but did you get that feeling? Did something seem 'not right at that moment? Trust those feelings. They are never wrong.

Perhaps you will need to sit with that lad for a few minutes and get interested in what he is doing. He may well have an explicit agreement with his partner that he gets $30 per week to gamble on the football, and she has access to the account to monitor it. That sort of thing is innocent fun.

But we also know that those Apps can be the doorway to someone's hell. It could be the thing that destroys their life and leads to suicide. But, on the other hand, when you take the time to get interested, your action may well be the thing that stops a disaster before it even starts.

You Never Know When an Opportunity Might Arise.

It is such a good thing to be able to help another human being. It is in our DNA to want to serve in this way. Along the way in my life, I have been given some golden opportunities to be of service. But, unfortunately, many of them I missed because I was either unaware or too selfish.

But then there were some magic moments. I want to share one with you.

In 2002, I was invited to run a 12 month-long educational program in Men's Health for Vietnam Veterans on the Mornington Peninsula.

I was given the material to present and could not align with it. So much of it was outdated, and I felt like it was designed to tell participants what to do rather than educating them and supporting them to learn and grow. So, I asked if I could present my material and was granted permission.

About the 6th visit, I walked into a room filled with anger, swearing and frustration. I watched for a while to experience what was unfolding, then asked one of the men in the front row to bring me up to speed.

Apparently, Veterans Affairs had changed some conditions on their benefits, and they were outraged. By the sound of it, the changes were minor, but the response was significant. So, I watched in disbelief for a while and decided that today's session would not go as planned.

I called their attention, and they quietened down, and I looked at them and said, "You blokes don't get it, do you? You just do not get it!" They looked at me, stunned as I stood silent for a bit.

"Here I am, a 42-year-old man with three kids, living in Australia, and wondering when I am going to stop feeling like a teenager and start feeling like a man, genuinely like a man. I yearn for an experience or a process that will challenge me enough to help me realise that mantle and feel fully confident in my masculinity and adulthood. Many of my friends are the same.

And here you all are a group of men who have faced life's most severe test. You stood and looked death in the eye and then walked toward it. You were forced to face your fear and your terror, and gain some ascendency over all of your weaknesses, and walk toward death, knowing this could be your very last walk.

Do you know how special that makes you guys? You have something I want, and I may never get it. You should be taking that out into the world to support young men who are struggling, to help them through. You should be taking that powerful guardianship you have out into the community to care for others, especially the vulnerable. And here you are, bitching and moaning like a bunch of entitled teenagers. I am disgusted with you! "

There was dead silence for a long time. I then ran the rest of the session.

The following week, 40% of them did not return, and I never saw most of those again. The rest, however, gave me some magical experiences as they stepped up in the world and began to serve for all they were worth. It was amazing.

Then, a couple of months later, another amazing thing happened.

At the local primary school, there was a fantastic teacher. He taught music and had been deeply kind to my son, who found school a bit of a struggle. I learned that two years after my son left the school, this man was finally appointed as Art Teacher, his first love.

The information triggered something for me. I knew there is an incredible link between creative expression and wellness. So, I decided to see if I could create an art class for my Vietnam Vets. I approached the teacher. He was both excited and nervous. I had a budget to pay him, so we set a date.

On the day, he was most apologetic that he did not have pottery wheels, but he forged ahead and taught some of the men how to work with clay, some of them painted, and others did other crafts. They loved it.

A week or so later, I received a long letter from Mick. Mick was the least popular group member because he would interrupt with long monologues and drive the others crazy. I used to take his interjections as an opportunity to learn patience and appreciation. Sometimes the blokes would yell at him to shut up.

This letter was true to form, but unlike his monologues, it was deeply beautiful. He shared how the art class had changed his life and how he had forgotten the joy of creating with his hands. He shared that he had been sleeping better and feeling more at peace.

Then he wrote that there was something stapled to the back of the letter that was to be given to the art teacher to buy pottery wheels. So, I checked and found five brand new, $100 notes.

He asked me to pass the money on, tell the teacher what it was for, but never inform him from where it came. He wrote that if he ever found out that the teacher learned the source of the money, he would hunt me down, and it would not be pretty.

So, I took the money to the school, went to the principal's office, and asked him to call the teacher. I handed over the money and said that I could not tell him where it came from, but it was inspired by his kindness to the veterans. He wept with joy, and the pottery wheels arrived two weeks later.

You never know when absolute magic will happen. What I have learned, though, if you live your life and seek to act with good intentions, it happens.

Consider the Benefits.

When we all become better at being more interested and aware of what is happening around us and attending to what is needed, our societies evolve and become better. People become safer in the streets, and children can safely play outside. Communities thrive.

In the workplace, the same thing happens. As a result, we reduce disconnectedness and loneliness, inclusion becomes routine, and workplace cultures become something that everyone wishes they were part of.

We cannot wait for Governments or Company Management to create these things. They cannot. They are created by the people on the ground deciding to grow, get better, and care for others.

Your kids and grandkids will grow up in a more peaceful and supportive world.

Females and Other Vulnerable Colleagues on Remote Sites

In a 60 Minutes episode titled "Lower than Low", which aired in the first half of 2022, the program highlighted the profound level of sexual harassment and abuse toward women on mine sites. They described it as almost being "the norm".

From an Australian Man's perspective this is hard to hear. I do not like the thought of my fellow countrymen acting in such an animalistic and barbaric way. But it is taking place, on a regular basis.

What I found to be even more disgusting is that often, when women complained, they were either ignored or fired. This is disgraceful beyond measure.

Young women who arrive at a mine site for the first time are often considered by groups of men to be "Fresh Meat". They are not considered to be some other man's daughter who needs to be respected and treated with care and reverence.

Women are subjected to demands for sexual favour to qualify for promotion to different roles. They have men, often bosses, exposing themselves, making lewd suggestions and touching and handling them inappropriately.

They then are faced with the indignity of being asked for proof and evidence if they make a complaint. They are not given the respect of being trusted as someone who is being truthful.

It gets worse. There are cases of supervisors who request sexual favours, when rejected, set about destroying the woman's career in the mines.

Often the mine site may not have cell phone reception and of course, there are no police. So, the mine site supervisors are the higher authority. This can leave some women in a precarious position where they have no power and no support. They are literally at the effect of their abusers.

And I should add here that it is not just women. Some vulnerable men suffer a similar fate in the form of bullying, often at the hands of those same male supervisors.

Multiple women have been raped in mining camps. Some, drugged and raped by more than one perpetrator. I could go on and on, but I think you get the picture.

Working remotely can be dangerous for women and vulnerable men.

You wonder how this could be? For a start, whilst women can match men in just about every area of life, they are not as physically strong. If a man wants to, he has a good chance of overpowering a woman. For two men, it is much easier.

A woman who is drugged has no chance against a man.

Further, I have come to realise that many men who are predatory towards women have chosen to work in the mines because, out there, they are out of site and away from law enforcement. They think they can get away with it.

Imagine for a moment, your sister or daughter going to work on a mine site where there is nobody looking out for her and there are predators there. It is a sick feeling.

So, I come back to the elements of care and guardianship.

Community Responsibility of Men on Remote Sites

I suggest to you that if you are a man, and you are living in a mining camp and working on a mine site, one of your civil responsibilities is the care of your female colleagues.

I cannot speak for you, but I can share how I feel.

If I was working on a mine site, and I had female colleagues, I would be checking in with them on a regular basis to ensure they feel both safe and comfortable. If they told me of any men who were being inappropriate, I would let my boss know, and then let my boss know I would be having a chat to the man in question.

I want to help him to step up and be a better and more respectful person.

Second, at night, I would make sure my female colleagues were safe in their accommodation before I retired. If I could not do it, I would ensure someone else did.

If I witnessed other men being gross and inappropriate toward women on the site, I would note which company they work for and report them to their employers and ask that they be helped; or removed.

I would never take any of this lightly.

And do not be put off by female colleagues who appear confident and at ease. They can still be targeted.

If you have female colleagues who decide to go and have a few drinks one evening, make sure they are cared for. They have as much right as anyone to socialise. But it is at times like this that drinks can be spiked. Make sure they get back to their accommodation safely.

Paul Roos tells me the story of when he was a young kid on the Fitzroy playing list. He and Gary Pert were mates from childhood and broke into the Fitzroy team at the same time.

He shared that they had brilliant experiences as young players because some of the older players were deeply good and responsible human beings.

He shared that, on their end-of-season trip, Michael Conlan and Laurie Serafini never went to bed until they first made sure that "Perty" and "Roosie" were in bed. They took care of them and kept them out of trouble.

On mine sites, if you are a capable man, this will be your "unpaid" responsibility. Take care of women and men who may be at risk of bullying. Keep them out of harm's way. If you do it well, the predators will move on because they will realise that they can no longer have their way on mine sites.

And if a female member is sexually harassed, compromised, or inappropriately handled by a supervisor, stand with her. Do not allow the event to be dismissed. Get your mates to stand with her. Make it clear to brutish supervisors that the team is bigger than they are when it needs to be.

For your own sense of self, for your own self-worth, do not ever step back and act like a powerless coward. You will hate yourself and will be justifying your actions till you die.

A Matter of Common Decency

I remember when I was a teenage boy, my mates and I were all obsessed with sex. We commented on girls we saw and talked about what we would like to do with them. We were treating them as nothing more than objects of our lust.

Perhaps that is what teenage boys go through when they are charged with testosterone. As a mate of mine Peter Shearer used to call it, "Testosterone is the 'fuck it' or 'kill it' hormone".

Of course, we did not behave like that within ear shot of any adults, so it was not as if anyone was there to teach us better, to help us to understand respect for women.

When I look back, I wonder how we would have received a talk from an adult we trusted, who might have assumed we were talking that way, and who wanted to help us with it.

But the reality of life catches up with the teenage mind and we sooner or later must grow up and become respectful men. Right!

In some cases, sadly that doesn't happen.

When I was 17 and doing year 12, I received a tough lesson from a classmate. And it was a good lesson. He was dating one of the girls in our year and I was keen to get the inside info on what she was like and if she was "putting out".

He looked at me and said, "Johnny, we don't talk about those things mate. Have you considered how disrespectful that would be to my girlfriend. You should never discuss those things with your mates."

I felt humiliated but I knew he was right. I have been eternally grateful for him having the courage to not simply reject my question, but to set me straight.

I am sure many men have never had someone say that to them. So, I am going to say it now.

Women are not there to be the objects of your animal lust. They are there to deliver their contribution to humanity in the best way they can, just as men are.

It does not matter who they are or what position they hold, they should be treated with care, respect, and reverence.

When you choose to treat women this way, you keep yourself out of the gutter too and restore your own dignity and your sense of decency. But it doesn't stop there.

We, as men, must help the men around us. Some of them are still stuck in their teenage thinking and feel that it is ok to treat women as objects of their animal lust. It is part of your role as a member of society to help them with that.

Some men revert to a sort of teenage boy mentality when they are around a group of men, especially if a few drinks are being consumed. They may need your support to shift them out of this place.

But you don't need to humiliate them in front of a group. If you have a man in your group who is being disrespectful to women in any way, take him for a walk and chat about it. Ask him how he would feel if another man talked about his daughter in the same way. Help him to remember that the women he just disrespected is a human being, someone's daughter, partner, sister, mother and that she deserves nothing more than his reverence, respect, and care.

We will only stop the predatory sexual abuse of women if we, as men, seek to be nothing but respectful, and to help our friends and colleagues to do the same.

Changing the world begins with changing ourselves.

Chapter Summary

It takes a village to raise a child or to guide a teenager. It also takes a community to support a person in need or has "gone off the rails".

We cannot be everything for our kids. Sometimes we have different interests and different paths. That is where our friends and other community members become so important.

Community Groups, Clubs and Societies are crucial for helping kids, teenagers and young adults find their way among people with similar interests.

You may need to face the fact that your child might not have any interest in the things about which you are most passionate.

In these settings, parents also get to help other parents. So, take notice of the things you notice.

There are places where parents unwittingly reveal they have tendencies to abuse their children or others. These people need help. Your help gives their kids great relief.

A single act of kindness and responsibility can change an entire community.

We can no longer stand by and do nothing about domestic violence.

"When men were being killed on the street, we took action. So why is domestic violence different?" by Karen Williams.

Reactive violence first must be stopped in our own minds.

Remember that your anger is arising in your universe whenever you find yourself reacting to a situation and getting angry. It is not coming from outside of you.

The use of intimidation to dominate others is ugly and violent.

If you or I still can feel rage, then we have a capacity for violence. Anger is healthy; rage signals a loss of control.

We must all learn to be more compassionate and understanding. If not, we will continue to hear of people dying brutally and senselessly.

What would happen if the entire world decided to stop treating violence with violence?

Do you dare to dream of a brighter future?

Domestic violence perhaps only remains a secret because good people refuse to notice the subtle signs they notice.

"The only thing necessary for the triumph of evil is for good men to do nothing." Edmund Burke

What we accept within ourselves, we will permit in our communities.

When I notice something that is not right around me, I must handle it or help.

Playing Right versus Wrong does not help anyone. We simply need to help people who are living in destructive ways.

When I seek to take care of an angry, raging man, I am most likely caring for his family too.

Where were Rowan Baxter's friends? Or were they hoping the government or authorities would be watching him?

The same goes too when women use the Family Law system to seek retribution against their spouses by dishonestly blocking equal access to their children. That, too, is a form of domestic violence.

When you see or hear evidence of domestic violence, you cannot walk away from it. However, you can either be part of the solution or become part of the problem by doing nothing.

Safe communities are places where citizens have guardianship for the welfare and safety of others.

Perhaps our challenge is to take our attention off our selfishness and place it on the welfare of our community and our environment.

Are you up for stepping up and doing what it takes to extract yourself from your mind and become an aware and available citizen who can stand as a guardian?

We all have minds. Minds can become full of quite crazy thoughts. Without the wise guidance of an open heart, we may follow the madness of our minds and descend into savagery and stupidity.

At work, we connect with many people, and we have the potential to notice many things.

When we are at work, we can have all our attention on ourselves, or we can direct it out into the world and take note of what is happening for the benefit of others.

When we are on a potentially dangerous site, every person has a unique and potentially helpful perspective.

When moving about at work, do you notice non-physical things that may indicate a risk to the wellbeing of a colleague – for example, the use of gambling apps.

Do you take note of things that are said that are "out of place"? Then, perhaps there is a chance to help someone.

Gambling can be one person's hobby and another person's doorway to hell.

The desire to help others, relieve suffering or improve circumstances for others is deeply encoded in our DNA.

Our selfishness can take away the profound gift we give ourselves when we take a moment to care for others. The result of helping is a strong sense of self, feeling good about who you are.

Remember my tales of the Vietnam Veterans. There are so many opportunities to do good. In these moments, you feel like you are living your life in a beautiful way.

All your good intentions and the actions you take have ripple effects. They improve workplace cultures, and they improve communities. They contribute to the improvement of societies.

If you want your grandchildren to grow up in a peaceful world, it starts with your next act of kindness.

Step up and care for the women and other vulnerable people on your site.

Do not stand for predators in positions of power preying on your female teammates.

Do whatever you can to make your work site a place that is safe for women, and unsafe for predatory men. It is your duty as a man and human being.

Work on yourself and help your friends and colleagues to become nothing but reverence, respectful and caring to all women.

Life Tips from This Chapter

Perhaps my first tip here is to ask yourself when you would like to step up in this world and begin acting like a responsible adult. We cannot remain rebellious teenagers all our lives.

If you are struggling in this area of your life, seek out a mentor.

Ask yourself about your sense of what is right and what is not acceptable. How would you have other people treat your children? How would you have other people treat your parents?

What are you prepared to accept? And what are you prepared to stand up to?

If you have lost your way in this area, then it may be time to embark upon some self-improvement. To do this, you can read some good books, or download the audio versions. Take your time working your way through them. Take notes and journal your thoughts.

Speak to some friends. Ask them if they would all like to start reading a book together and discuss the chapters as you go, sharing perspectives on what you have learned. It is nice to be supported on such a quest.

I recommend a book as a start point and have mentioned it more than once in this book. The book is titled, "The Road Less Travelled", by M. Scott Peck.

There are great self-development courses you can do. It depends on how ready you are to take your life on and become the person you would like to be.

There is a 2 Day workshop you can do, that is delivered via zoom over 3 or 4 sessions, called ReSurfacing®. It is a non-confronting step into some excellent self-development. You can learn about it at the following link.

https://tinyurl.com/Resurfacer

Taking Care of Home Base

Whilst you are away at work, there is a world that continues at home. You may have a partner at home, perhaps with kids. It is crucial for your peace of mind and productivity at work that your home base is well set up and functions smoothly.

I am aware that often this is not the case. It is heartbreaking to hear about workers who pick up their phone at lunchtime to read a text that says, "You need to come home immediately" while onsite and busy working.

Such a situation creates high levels of distress and can be a powerful distraction that could lead to accidents and injury.

People working on mining and construction projects are operating in potentially dangerous environments. So many things can go wrong, so workers need to have a clear mind and focus on the job.

Battling stresses at home can consume one's attention and dull their awareness. It can take away one's ability to sleep restfully.

Is your situation at home fully set up to support you whilst you are away? And are you doing what is needed to help keep things stable at home?

Creating Agreements

Agreements are powerful if made with commitment and sincerity. They provide a stable foundation upon which things can be built, including relationships.

When you decided to become a FIFO worker, did you sit with your partner and discuss it to ensure they were entirely "on board" when you applied for your role? Or did you submit your application first and tell them later?

It is important to note that it is never too late to create a new agreement.

When creating such an agreement, you are expressing all your thoughts, both of you, about what is needed, what your expectations are, and what you feel you can and cannot do.

It is crucial to bring everything out in the open. What are the collective obligations, like paying bills, caring for children, tasks around the house, caring for ageing parents, community responsibilities and many other things?

When it is all open and transparent, you can set to work with your partner creating agreements about who will do what, how things will get done and what will be your backup plans if things change or fail to turn out as planned.

To make things work, all you need to do is hold up your end of the bargain, keep your agreements, and be honest if ever you have a challenge with doing so.

Everyone is different. I know that I can be forgetful sometimes, so I put things into my phone calendar as a reminder. Part of keeping my agreements involves me making sure that I do not forget. It is not someone else's role to remind me.

Part of your agreements should be around establishing a support structure for the home-based partner when challenges arise that may be overwhelming.

Setting Up a Support Structure

If your partner is at home and has others to care for, like children or ageing parents, sometimes they may need support, and you will not be there to help them out.

So, what will you/they do?

Who can you or they call upon to be there for support when needed?

This situation requires an explicit agreement. It can be serious. For example. What happens if your partner, while caring for kids, receives a call to say that an ailing parent has been rushed to the hospital? They cannot just leave the kids to be with their or your parent.

A backup support plan is needed. Who can you create a support agreement with who is prepared to drop everything and be there so that your partner can move quickly?

If your children are young, you may well need more than one person there as your backup support. Therefore, it is crucial to predict all possible scenarios to ensure you can make a call and put a plan into action when needed.

When you fail to put support structures in place, you will likely receive a message at work that will leave you feeling powerless and stressed.

Who are the people in your life you completely trust and know on whom you can depend? It may be a sibling, a neighbour, a close friend or even a parent. The people you choose mustn't let you down.

It is also helpful to understand that this sort of thing is coded into our DNA. We are community-based beings, and we gain enrichment when we get a chance to help others out. It is part of our innate desire to serve our community.

It would undoubtedly be helpful to you to make sure you keep the ledger well balanced and help others whenever you can. You may recall a familiar adage, "The more we give, the more we tend to receive." But it is crucial to realise that giving with the expectation of receiving is not giving; It is manipulating.

Keeping Your Relationship Strong and Vibrant

If your relationship is not strong, you will create anxiety, stress, and sleepless nights for yourself. Further, whilst you are at work, worry will take your mind off the job and put you, the job, and your colleagues at risk.

Some of you do dangerous work, or you are the partner of someone doing dangerous work. It is so important that those who are doing hazardous work are not experiencing anxiety around their relationships.

This is so important.

Every doubt, mistrust or miscommunication can become mental cancer that can destroy a life. Therefore, you must conduct yourself with honour in your relationship and care for your partner's feelings.

And remember, you are both human beings. Therefore, it is essential to "cut each other some slack" and allow for off days, negative moods that may arise from fatigue, loneliness, discouragement, or external challenges.

Sometimes, choosing to be offended by what your partner says or does, is as significant as the offensive statement or action. An old parenting mentor of mine once told me, "Do not try to engage your kids' cooperation when they are either tired, sick, hungry or stressed. They are operating in reptile brain mode."

When you or your partner are tired, sick, hungry, or stressed, you will be in reptile brain mode. It is vitally important to be aware of that because sometimes, your partner will say things to you that are reactive and not meant to hurt. If you see that for what it is, you will be ok. You can be a bit like a batsman who ducks under the bouncer and allows it to go through to the keeper.

Choosing to be offended can be a doorway to anguish, anger, and a whole raft of negative emotions.

It Takes Effort

What can you do each day to uplift your partner? How can you encourage your partner daily?

Have you got your partner's back?

In my life, I have been passionate about supporting my partner and friends to go for their hopes and dreams. Every person on the planet has the right to explore their inspiration and go for a big goal.

As a partner, I choose to support that, help out where I can, give them a push if they need it, always be encouraging and support them through their disappointments. And all the while, ready to celebrate their wins with them.

If you intend to continually help your partner become the "very best person" they can be, you will have a good life. And this does not mean you have the right to admonish them or make them wrong when they make a mistake or go off the rails a little. Nobody enjoys being made wrong.

But you can seek to understand and support your partner to get back on track with strength and love. Remember, your partner is a human being.

Put Yourself in Your Partner's Shoes

You have your life, and your partner has theirs. You are entirely familiar with your daily existence. You may think you know your partner's everyday existence, but all you know is what you see. You have never experienced it.

My suggestion to you is to take more interest. Talk about it. Share feelings and listen with interest and curiosity, and seek to understand. If you think you know, you will breach trust.

We can all take a lesson from Darryl Kerrigan in "The Castle". He and his wife had this extraordinary admiration, respect, and reverence for each other. No wonder his quotes have become folklore.

When your partner makes a mistake, or even when they do the wrong thing, remember that you too have made mistakes in your life. There have been times when you did wrong. It is ok. Human beings are not perfect creatures, but we can all learn.

Having compassion for your partner will place you in a position where you can be more connected, understanding, and helpful. As a result, you will build trust.

I have an old friend. He never did enjoy school. He is a brilliant artist who could not quite get his head around all the other subjects at school and was often bored. Sometimes, his boredom saw him wander off and do things that got him into trouble. For example, playing with fire one day, he burned down a large shed. Picking him up for the Police Station, his Mum put her arm around him and said what she always said at times like this. "Don't worry, mate. It's just a bad day!"

He told me that those words got him through his teenage years and into adulthood, where he became a brilliantly successful and internationally recognised artist.

Trust is Essential.

I was having a conversation with a woman not too long ago. I had met her recently and was inquiring about her life. I am always most interested in people, and I love to learn about their lives.

She began to tell me about the failure of her marriage and how her ex-husband had cheated on her. She said she was not able to forgive him for such a shocking breach of trust.

I find this to be a typical scenario, so I asked her a question. "What were your marriage vows?" She looked at me and said, "I do not know. That was a long time ago. So why do you ask?"

I shared that I find it fascinating that our marriage vows are probably the first time in our lives where we declare to the world how we are going to be, what we are going to do and how we are going to conduct ourselves. It is a moment when we make a solemn pledge. So, I shared I am amazed that most people have no recollection of their marriage vows.

I then went on and shared that one common vow is to love and honour our partner. If ever we have engaged in criticism, abuse, disrespect, ridicule, or any related action, then we have broken our solemn oath.

As I contemplated this topic in my own life, I knew I had breached my vows many times. Of course, it takes a great deal of effort to honour lofty vows. But a breach is a breach and needs to be amended.

So, I asked this lady if she had ever breached her marital vows? I said that I understand her hurt connected with her husband's breach but had she ever broken her solemn vow.

She called me a few days later and said, "Thank you for our chat. I got to realise how awful I was to my husband at times. I realise that I had not honoured my marriage vows. So I do not feel angry at him anymore and feel more connected to him. It will be a relief for our kids."

I want to remind you again. You are both human beings. You will make mistakes, and you will do dumb things. Seek to be understanding. However, "I am only human" can never be your excuse. You must own your own mistakes. However, taking the attitude to your partner that they are human and prone to errors gives them the space they need to own their mistakes.

Remember, when you make someone wrong, they become defensive and shut down. Therefore, communication is not possible from that place.

In the next chapter, I talk about "Striking when the iron is cold", a powerful skill that gets everyone out of the heat of the moment. It is not possible to have a rational discussion when you are either angry or reactive. Such a situation is a pathway to conflict and regret. Do not go there.

Sharing your intimacy

I understand that this is an area that can be sensitive. But I feel that it is crucial.

Back in the '90s, I read "Kosher Sex" by Shmuley Boteach, a New York Rabbi. He talked about the importance of keeping all your sexual behaviour for your partner.

Note: Some might think it odd that I read this book as I was raised a Catholic. However, after I finally extracted myself from my catholic upbringing, I read more from other belief systems.

Rabbi Boteach went as far as to say that you should not ever masturbate when away from your partner but resist the desires and wait for when you are together. He shared that it creates a much closer bond and a more profound connection during lovemaking.

He is not coming from a moral platform. Instead, he offers his readers tools for building a stronger, richer, and more enduring relationship.

I am aware that Rabbi Boteach wrote this book well before mobile phones and the powerful internet-based media resources we have access to, including Skype, Zoom and FaceTime. I am also aware he was probably talking to an audience who might be separate from their partners for short periods on a semi-regular basis, like those travelling for business. Perhaps he did not consider the plight of FIFO workers who are continually away from their partners for more than two weeks at a time.

I raise this because I believe there is a trap into which many have fallen.

Porn!

Boredom, loneliness, and animal level urges can culminate as intense levels of desire that interfere with sleep and create an unwanted distraction. Many people turn to masturbation when they are away from their partners. It is normal.

However, if you are using pornography as inspiration for your solo session, then you may be creating somewhat of a wall between you and your partner, mainly if your partner is not aware of what you are doing.

When you engage in porn without your partner knowing, you break trust and create something you are forced to hide. These two things, breaching trust and hiding things, can break down your capacity to connect honestly and openly with your partner.

I want to make it clear that I am not making a value judgement here. I am not a fan of porn, mostly because I have read about the porn industry and know that many actors are desperate people who are sacrificing everything just to get money. However, I have also learned that an alarmingly high percentage of people working in the porn industry were once victims of child sexual abuse.

My invitation to you is to be completely open with your partner. Share your intimacy with them. You have Skype, FaceTime and many other avenues for live, face to face connection. This keeps you together and prevents actions that may cause separation.

You Are Part of Something Bigger

My parents were married for nearly 50 years before my Dad died. Of course, they had their challenges and their tough times, but their loyalty to each other was strong.

There were times when my Dad's drinking, and his efforts to give up smoking, made him intolerable. He could be angry and aggressive. However, two things kept them together.

First, my mother was a patient, kind and forgiving woman. She always had space in her heart to forgive.

The second was their shared desire to contribute to their greater community, to make things better in the world for those less fortunate.

Whilst we ran pubs, they tirelessly raised money for a Boy's Orphanage, cared for the elderly in the community, and always put on a Christmas Lunch for the older people in our neighbourhood who had nowhere to go on Christmas Day. I remember those lunches with much warmth as our family served the meals and ensured everyone had a wonderful day.

Outside of that, they were always involved in local sporting clubs as coaches, administrators, and helpers. So when we moved into the Windsor Hotel in Miles in Queensland in the mid-'60s, my Dad realised there was an excellent social opportunity when he discovered the old, abandoned horse racing track. Within a year, Miles had a thriving racing club that brought the entire community together.

These actions they engaged in raised their self-esteem and kept them together and aligned. They were working together on something much bigger than each of them as individuals and as a couple.

When you are both inspired by something much more expansive and out in front of you, then you tend to live your life side-by-side. However, when your primary focus is your relationship, you spend too much time toe-to-toe.

My question for you is: "What is something that you and your partner can be involved in that will bring value to others?"

What can you do together that will leave you feeling good about your life? It may be something that improves your local community. But, on the other hand, it may be something that relieves the suffering of people less fortunate.

I always remember my Grandpa. He was a profoundly wonderful man. Whilst he was never religious, his wife, my Grandma, was an active member of her church community and took care of the flower arrangements on the alters and around the church. The flowers were always fabulous.

My Grandpa grew the flowers. He was retired but worked tirelessly in the garden to produce extraordinary flower crops so that my Grandma could do her thing.

And as an aside, when my Grandpa rose at 5:00 am every morning to water his gardens, he first made two cups of tea and sat on the bed to enjoy time with his wife before starting his day. Those little things are so important.

Gratitude for Your Partnership

There are so many lonely people in the world right now. Some of you who are reading this book are single and perhaps experiencing a degree of loneliness.

If you are in a relationship, have you stopped for a moment to feel gratitude for what you have.

Many of us get caught up in thinking about what is wrong with our relationship, how it could be better or why our partner is not who we want them to be. We can get caught up in our righteousness about some petty squabble and allow ourselves to forget that this is the person with whom we fell deeply in love.

Taking time out to allow yourself to experience gratitude helps to alleviate these feelings. Taking time to write, every day if you need to, all the things about your partner you are grateful for is healing.

Suppose you practice gratitude for your partner and your relationship. In that case, when you connect to talk, you will meet through the eyes of appreciation instead of the displeasure of resentment.

If you have a relationship and it is in reasonable shape, you are one of the lucky ones. It would be wise for you to appreciate that.

Creating Workable Routines

You are not just trying to survive this. This is your life. Let us work to make it great. What did John Lennon Say?

Many people do get lost in thinking about the future or the past. For example, they often take on a job and decide they do not like it, but they will endure it for a few years because of the money or convenience.

That is a wrong attitude. This is your life, right here, right now. How are you going to make it work for you so that it is fulfilling and enjoyable? I am talking to you, the worker, and you, the person at home waiting for your partner.

Routines and Clear Agreements

Creating clear and workable agreements, about who does what and when, makes a home run smoothly. When no agreements are in place, things fall apart, and normally one person starts to feel like a law enforcement officer as they seek to get others to contribute.

Tension, conflict, and resentment follow.

Putting the Kids to Work

When my kids were little, we gave them chores to do around the house. There were a variety of jobs that included:

- Feeding the dogs
- Bringing wood in for the fire
- Tidying the lounge
- Taking out the garbage
- Taking out the compost
- Tidying their rooms.

We did not have a system where they were paid for their jobs or fine them for not doing their job. So we talked with them about providing valuable service in the home, doing their bit to keep everything moving.

Over the following weeks, we found ourselves constantly having to remind them and regularly striking incredible resistance as they tried their best to avoid their tasks because they had "better" things to do.

As a kid, I remember being too scared of my Dad to avoid a chore. So, I got into them quickly to get them out of the way. But I was not going to use fear with my kids.

We then tried something that worked. We talked with the kids again about the jobs they were going to be doing. We then asked them to write up their agreement to do those tasks and to sign it. We then placed it on the fridge.

If a task was not completed, we asked, "Are you going to fulfil your agreement?" And they did.

It was such an excellent system because all we had to do was remind them of the agreements they had made.

Managing Tasks at Home
If you are in a relationship and want things to work smoothly at home, then it can be an excellent idea to decide who will take responsibility for what and when.

There are tasks to be done inside the house and jobs to be completed outside the home. Some are regular because they have a due date, like putting out bins and paying bills, and others can vary due to other influences like lawn moving and garden weeding or gutter cleaning.

How smoothly could your home run if everyone had their duties, an easy-to-read timetable, and a commitment to doing their bit? Then, while you are not there, your partner would feel supported.

If you have kids, they will be building self-esteem because they are doing their bit, keeping agreements and doing something of value for others.

When you return from your shift, it also means that you know what you need to do around the house. It helps you to slip back into the routine of life in the home.

For example, you might have a list of tasks that are regularly yours when at home. They might be things like:

- Cook the dinner each night.
- Mow the lawns.
- Check the gutters and clean if necessary.
- Bottle the Kombucha and prepare the next batch.

Every 2 months, you might have tasks like:

- Clean the Windows on the outside.
- Trim the path edges.
- Clean the Oven.

It does not matter what the tasks are. What matters is the family coming together to share the load, create agreements and then committing to keeping those agreements. When you do this sort of thing, you are teaching your kids excellent values and self-discipline.

You may even decide to put it all into an Excel spreadsheet and have everyone enter their tasks into their reminders on their mobile phone.

Relationship Routines
Putting things into place that you and others can look forward to is helpful and uplifting.

For example, you remember your partner is the person you love. You fell in love with this person. It can be most enriching to have a designated "date night". Perhaps you can take it in turns to take responsibility for what Date Night looks like - but knowing that it is an immovable date in the calendar creates a positive connection and a closeness.

The same can go with your kids. For example, you may have a child who is mad about football, fishing, or skateboarding. So you can organise a "date event" with each of them too.

My son loved Skate Boarding. We regularly visited different Skate Parks*. My job was to get him there and to stay for as long as he wanted to stay. I would take a book and read, or sometimes watch. It was an enjoyable thing for both of us.

Perhaps it is a regular seat at the football when you are home or sharing time working on a different hobby. These are the things your kids look forward to and will make your return home less routine for them and more of something to anticipate.

*** A Note about Skate Parks**. Have you ever been to one? They are amazing. I have never seen anything work as they do. The kids are respectful, and everyone gets their turn. Nobody gets to dominate, no matter how skilled you are. Big kids take care of little kids. It is beautiful. Workplaces across the world could learn a lot from Skate Parks.

Coming Home is Not Your Holiday

There is an interesting thing that happens to some folks who travel for work. There can be a sense that whilst you have been away, doing it tough on your own, bringing in the money, that you are entitled to have a few days break.

On the one hand, I understand that. But on the other hand, it is profoundly selfish and destructive.

While you were away working, even if your partner does not have formal employment, they have kept the home-front running. They have kept things in order so you may keep your attention on your work.

When you come home, sure you will be entitled to some recreation, but you also must do your bit. If you have young children, for example, your partner might need a break.

This is your life. It is what you signed up to. It is not two weeks on and then one week holiday. It is two weeks away, one week at home.

You do not "deserve" anything just because you have been away.

And if you are the home-based partner, you do not "deserve" anything simply because you have been holding things together whilst your partner is away.

As soon as you believe you "deserve", then you are no longer a team. Being an effective team takes work, sacrifice, respect, and continuous commitment to something bigger than you.

Suspicion, Mistrust and Broken Agreements

Do not create things you feel you need to keep secret from your partner. Secrets create separation. You may be able to hide it, but you will not be able to hide its presence. Your partner will feel that something is amiss.

Being honest, straightforward, and transparent is the key to creating relationships that are trusting and free of suspicion.

If you break an agreement or drop your end of an agreement, own up immediately. Take responsibility. Do not justify or blame. Just own it and repair the damage.

These actions build trust and remove suspicion.

A Note for The Single Worker

You, too, can have agreements with yourself about what you will do when you get home. A plan creates productivity and valuable use of time and resources.

When you have no plans, you are likely to waste a lot of time and succumb to boredom.

What can you contribute to your community? Are there sports clubs that need a hand? Can you take on a productive hobby? What can you contribute?

Chapter Summary

If you have a partner and family at home, you must have things sorted there for your peace of mind at work.

You never want to receive stressed and urgent "You need to come home now!" texts while working remotely.

Unrest at home creates distress at work and puts you at risk of mistakes.

Have you got suitable support structures in place?

Agreements are the bedrock of a stable life.

If you do not have clear agreements with your partner and your children, it is not too late to create them.

What is needed? What do you need? What does your partner need? What do your kids need?

Bring everything into the open, including obligations and responsibilities. Nothing hidden.

From here, you can create agreements and backup plans.

Keep your agreements. If ever you feel you cannot, then talk about it ahead of time. Communicate.

Do what you need to do to ensure you remember what you have agreed to do and when.

Support structures are crucial for when things happen at home, and you are not there to help.

Take this seriously. Who can you depend upon to care as much as you do, to show up as you would, in the case of an emergency?

Predict what may happen, and then have a clear plan in place when it comes to your kids, a backup for your backup.

Choose people who will not let you down.

Do not forget to do your bit and help out wherever you can. Keep your ledger well balanced.

Strong relationships prevent worry and poor sleep. Weak relationships can do the opposite.

Worry and anxiety whilst doing dangerous work can be fatal.

Conduct yourself with honour in your relationship and take care of your partner's feelings.

Remember to cut each other some slack. You are human beings.

Taking offence at something is often as bad as being offensive. So, patience and understanding are your keys.

Sometimes your partner is tired or stressed. Allow for that. Pick things up tomorrow.

Make a daily effort to uplift, encourage and be supportive to your partner.

Nobody enjoys being made wrong.

Be prepared to put yourself into your partner's shoes. Have an appreciation for what is happening in their life.

Learn to take more interest and listen to understand. Ask questions. Give your partner the green light to talk. Everyone likes to feel heard. Listening with interest builds trust.

Remember. Everyone has a bad day from time to time.

Trust is essential. You can build trust by keeping your agreements and being reliable.

If you are married, what were your wedding vows? Have you kept them?

Remembering your partner is a human being and may make mistakes, helps to stop you from being reactive. But when you make a mistake, "I am only human" is not a valid excuse. Make amends.

Strike when the Iron is Cold.

Share your intimacy. Being away from your partner for two weeks can be challenging. Solo sex may not be a great idea. Connect with each other.

Connecting this way is a healthy strategy to prevent you from choosing porn, which can destroy you.

You are a human being, not an animal. It is good to behave like one. Succumbing to low-level desires and turning to porn means you have something to keep secret from your partner.

Take the time to become completely open with your partner.

Part of the glue that keeps a relationship strong is both parties being committed to something bigger than your relationship. Is there a cause that interests you?

Where are you needed in the community?

What is broken in the world that you both would like to see fixed?

What can you work on together to make the world better?

"When you are inspired by something much bigger and out in front of you, then you tend to live your life side-by-side. When your major focus is your relationship, you spend too much time toe-to-toe."

How can you support your partner's passion?

If you are in a relationship, are you feeling grateful for it?

What are the things in your relationship that are "right", "wonderful", "incredible"?

Enduring a situation because it has advantages is not suitable for your wellbeing. So how can you find a way to like it?

Creating clear and workable agreements about who does what and when makes a home run smoothly.

If you have kids, give them some responsibility. For example, create task agreements with them.

Creating written agreements with your kids can work well.

Dividing up tasks and creating a schedule helps to ensure that everything gets done with no conflict or blaming.

A schedule helps you to slip back into a routine when you arrive home from your shift. You then know what needs doing.

Relationship routines are so important with your partner and with each of your kids. Perhaps even with your close friends.

Go and check out a skate park. Witness the mutual support, the patience, and the care.

Coming home from your shift is not your holiday. You need to step into life at home and pick up the slack.

As soon as you think you "deserve" something, you are no longer a team player.

Keep your nose clean and be responsible. Do not create reasons why your partner might lose trust in you. Keep your agreements.

If you are single, manage yourself well. Have things to attend to when you return home from your shift.

Life Tips from This Chapter

Creating Agreements is not a flippant thing. Both parties need to have their full attention on what they are doing and make a clear commitment. The first serious agreement we often make is a marriage vow, but many put them aside and forget about them once the party is over.

Bring your marriage vows out regularly and refresh your commitment to them.

If the agreements are challenging, like they can be when one partner is choosing to start a career as a FIFO worker, then it might be helpful to seek the support of someone you both trust, to help create the agreement and then witness it. This could be a good friend, a religious minister or both of your parents.

If you are to bring a person in, you both need to create an agreement with the person that they will hold you to your agreement in the spirit it was made and never to take sides.

There is a wonderful book called "The Four Agreements" by Don Miguel Ruiz. It is a small book and is easy to read. Your kids will enjoy it too.

Getting Better at Self Care

Anyone who is going to take on a job should make sure they are in a reasonable state of fitness and health to handle the demands of that job. Most FIFO jobs are demanding due to the intensity of the workload, or the length of shifts, or both.

Are you as fit and healthy as you could be? If not, that is ok. You can always get better. But, before you start, it is nice to understand better how your body works, why it gets weak or sick, and how you can keep it in good condition. Understanding gives you power.

A Mass of Confusion

Over the past 100 years, human health has been turned into a complex and confusing set of theories that rarely align with each other, making it almost impossible to understand.

Perhaps the start point was when medical scientists turned the body into a set of diverse systems. You have heard of them: Skeletal System; Cardiovascular System; Respiratory System; Endocrine System; Digestive System; Nervous System; Reproductive System; Lymphatic System and Muscular System.

Medicine divided itself up into specialists for each system. As a result, we began to look at human health in a weird and disjointed way. Over the past 80 years, we have seen general health decline as obesity rates have climbed. Type 2 diabetes has reached almost epidemic levels, and many more people are getting sick and dying from a variety of cancers.

Every year, the cost of providing healthcare in Australia increases at a rate ahead of inflation. So we spend more and more on healthcare, and yet the population gets more and more unhealthy. Do not you look at that and ask questions?

Would you agree to spend more and more on your car insurance every year even though your cover continually diminished?

Our healthcare system rolls on without question. But we cannot deny the one blinding reality. Australians, like many other people from wealthy countries, are becoming more and more unhealthy.

What Happened with Covid-19?

When Covid-19 hit, Governments across the world did their modelling and decided to shut down the economy. It happened in Australia. From my interactions with many people, I realise the government did not articulate their actions very well because few understood why. As a result of this misunderstanding, governments were roundly criticised.

There was only one reason for the lockdowns, and it had nothing to do with the death rate.

You might remember the term "flattening the curve". It was the all-important factor. Governments across the world were frightened that their healthcare systems would collapse. If too many people fell ill from this new virus, the hospitals would not have coped.

Our Hospitals are already being stretched to breaking point with the general levels of ill health in our community. A surge in Corona Virus cases could have led to rioting in emergency departments.

And people criticised it. They raved on about 'not that many people dying' and 'it is not as bad as they predicted, but they did not understand this one big pressure point.

Governments worldwide are realising that we cannot do healthcare the same as we have always done it.

The Current State of Health in Australia

Dr Richard Carmona, the 17th Surgeon General of the USA, stated during a presentation I attended once, "The USA spends 19% of GDP on healthcare, and 80% of that is spent treating completely preventable diseases."

When questioned about the diseases he was referring to as "completely preventable", he answered: Cardiovascular diseases, most cancers, diabetes, most gastro-intestinal disorders, arthritis, and some autoimmune diseases.

The situation is the same in Australia. Our collective attitude to these ailments is not helpful. We see them as things that happen to us. We do not choose to know that we are continually creating the conditions for these diseases by living as we do.

Collectively, we do not exercise enough, we overeat, and way too much of what we eat is destructive to our health. We couple this with overconsumption of alcohol and drugs, add liberal amounts of stress, worry and poor sleep, and you have a recipe for pharmaceutical company profits.

Unlike some, I do not blame drug companies. They are businesses that seek to optimise their product sales. They want to make a profit. As consumers, we do not have to buy from them. We can change it.

But on the same note, huge profits are being made in healthcare without any genuine advances in medicine.

And why are there no genuine advances in medicine?

Degeneration as a Disease

All the disease or illness conditions I outlined earlier are degenerative. That means there is an ongoing level of degeneration in people's bodies – in your body.

When you were born, your body was perfect. It was ready to grow into a healthy and robust human being. Occasionally people are born with a genetic challenge, but nowhere near as many as seems to be reported. It is probably well below one-hundredth of 1% of cases.

I have a friend who is morbidly obese. I watch the way he lives, and it is no surprise. He is a wonderful man, but when I asked him about his weight, he said to me, "It is a genetic condition. There is nothing I can do about it". The explanation that followed made no sense to me at all. His idea of his weight being genetic permits him to eat incredible amounts of food, with loads of sweets to boot.

Since the second world war, there has been so much change that our day-to-day life is breaking our bodies down into disease. These changes have included:

- Huge increase in sugar consumption

- An extraordinary increase in the volume of chemicals used in food production
- Major advances in food processing, including the use of preservatives and additives.
- Soft drink replacing water as the primary beverage
- Significant increase in the levels of pollutants in the air
- A more sedentary lifestyle
- An increasing reliance on pharmaceutical medicine and alcohol
- Smoking
- Medical misconceptions about the origins of certain diseases leading to a further reduction in responsibility and long-term reliance on drugs that may not have been helpful.
- The over-use of antibiotics.

It is not the purpose of this book to be deeply prescriptive about exercise, nutrition, sleep, disease prevention and about other significant health enhancement factors.

Stay tuned for my next book that will show you how to navigate your way to exceptional health and wellbeing.

The Importance of Sleep

When I started doing my work in fatigue prevention, industry employers had made significant errors by assuming that fatigue was all about sleep. Of course, many factors create fatigue, but there is no doubt that sleep is an integral part of the equation.

There are many questions and mysteries around sleep. Some people get by on 4 to 5 hours per night. Some feel they need 9. Some people like a light on, and others require a fan. Some need it to be silent, and others have a special pillow. Some folks need their teddy? Some questions for you.

- What is enough sleep in your mind?
- How much sleep do you get?
- What time do you go to bed?
- Do you have trouble getting up in the mornings?
- Do you sleep in on the weekends?

- Do you snore?
- Do you have a set routine before retiring at night?

What is Sleep?

What is it? It is hard to describe it from personal experience because when we are asleep, we are unaware. When we sleep, we are in a state of reduced activity; resting. Therefore, we are less responsive to external stimuli.

Scientists tend to define sleep in terms of brain wave activity. There are three primary stages:

Before we go into this, I want to explain a term to you. REM Sleep. Rapid Eye Movement sleep is the deepest form of sleep. We go through three stages when we are headed into sleep.

- Wakefulness – High Brain Activity
- Non-Rem sleep – Low Brain Activity
- Rem sleep – High Brain Activity – Dream state

Brain Waves

What are they and how do they relate to sleep?

- Beta – Normal Waking state
- Alpha – Single Point of Focus
- Theta – Normal Sleep
- Delta – Very Deep Sleep or Deep Meditation

Beta: These predominate in our normal working day, and are necessary for logical thinking, multitasking of activities and the general managing of the day. It can be excessive and stressful where your head gets full of competing thoughts, all vying for your attention.

Alpha: Are generated where there is a single point of focus, and outside distractions do not disturb this singularity of focus.

Theta: Theta is the zone of the most creative thoughts. Theta is the Brainwave most associated with inspirational thinking and creativity. It is where the aha's are generated.

Delta: These are our deepest brainwaves and are in the unconscious mind. They bring us that sense of intuition, sixth sense and empathy. It is where that 'gut feeling' that often proves to be correct is recognised. To get to Delta, you need to start by moving toward Alpha with a single point of focus. It is the origin of the concept of "counting sheep". When you are tired, you usually find your way there easily. However, if you are too alert or your mind is a little stirred up, a single point of focus activity can help.

Body Temperature:
Body Temperature drops by up to 1 degree Celsius when we sleep, which reduces energy demand and helps us to sleep. Our body temperature decreases the most during REM sleep. If your bedroom is too warm, it is difficult for your body to create this drop in temperature.

Sleep-Wake Cycles and Circadian Rhythms
The Human body goes through rhythmic cycles of all types. Circadian Rhythms are the cycle of sleep/wake and light/dark. When it is Dark, the body wants to sleep.

Sleeping when it is Light can be a big challenge for most people except teenagers. Although, I must admit I was never able to pull that one-off. When it is light, and you need to sleep, you must prepare.

Forcing wakefulness when it is dark is also a big challenge and must be appropriately managed.

What is a desirable Rhythm?

What factors can interrupt a desirable Rhythm?

- Alcohol can stop you from going into your first REM Cycle.
- Exposing yourself to light in the middle of the night can interfere with your cycles. Get good at going to the bathroom in the dark; or have a very dull nightlight if that is too challenging.
- The blue light of common cellular devices can have a drastic impact on your sleep wake cycles. When you go to bed, place the phone face down, out of your reach.

It is amazing how you adapt and how your body does it. You have heard the term internal body clock. Ever notice how you tend to wake just before your alarm? That is your body timing its rise out of REM Sleep into non-REM sleep, right up to the lightest phase of non-REM sleep just before you are due to wake. If this is not happening for you most of the time, then there will be things you can do to improve your sleep.

Creating a Sleep Pattern

Here is a set of questions to help you plan your sleep.

- How much sleep do you feel you need? Look at the number of hours that tend to have you wake feeling deeply rested.
- What time do you need to get out of bed in the morning?
- How long does it take you to wake up?
- What time do you need to go to bed? Consider how long it normally takes for you to fall asleep.
- What time do you need to prepare to go to bed?

Once you answer these questions, you will know what time you need to commence your bed preparation.

Here is an example:
I need to be up at 5 am, and I do need 8 hours of sleep. But, I like to lay in for about 15 minutes before I get up. So I need to set my alarm for 4:45 am. So, I need to be asleep by 8:45 pm, but I will shoot for 8:30 to be sure.

When I go to bed, it usually takes me 15 minutes to fall asleep. My pre-bed routine of getting clothes ready for tomorrow, brushing teeth and so on takes me about half an hour. So, I need to be in bed by 8:15, so I should start preparing for bed at 7:45 pm.

Creating a Sleep Environment

Your room needs to be dark; the darker, the better. When it is dark, your body will want to sleep. Your brain picks up the signal that it is dark and will move you toward sleep. If you live in a very bright location, do your best to darken your room using blinds and perhaps even tape.

Having a television in your room goes against good sleep. The blue-white light stimulates you and interferes with your natural rhythms. If you have a TV in your quarters in a mining camp, turn it off at least an hour before sleep.

Sound is also a factor. How noisy is it where you live? Could there be less noise? Some people live in noisy places and adapt. I grew up living on Hoddle Street in Collingwood. Cars on one side, train tracks on the other. We got used to it, and it all became background noise.

Temperature is crucial. Remember, your body temp drops up to 1 degree while you sleep. It is as if it is creating the feeling of needing to be kept warm under some covering. Be mindful when warming a cold environment, not making it too hot. Sometimes on a cold night, people can overheat their homes just to avoid that moment of discomfort when disrobing and getting into bed. The downside is a hot room that may prevent body temperature from dropping adequately to provide good quality REM Sleep.

Moving air is often helpful, which can be achieved by opening a window or using a fan.

You will also need some Rules and agreements with your partner.

What is your bed for – sleep and intimate connection? Reading in bed is restful and helpful for calming the mind.

What can you discuss in bed? Not the relationship. Not money. Not stressful things. Talk about those things at the kitchen table and resolve them before retiring.

Do not go to bed halfway through an incomplete argument. Sometimes you must decide to stop wanting to be correct and concede and create peace. It takes courage, but it keeps your relationship strong.

You may also add to the sleep environment:

- Deeply relaxing and meditative music.
- White noise like rain or water flowing. (Apps like Rain Rain give you these)
- Essential Oils

Snoring and Sleep Apnoea

Both of these conditions can be repaired. Snoring reduces the quality of your sleep, disturbs others, and most often, you do not know you are doing it.

Sleep Apnoea is far worse. You lose the desire to breathe in and stop breathing. It can be frightening to watch someone with sleep apnoea, as you wonder if they will inhale.

Breathing is controlled by your Inspiratory Control Centre in the brain. It is sensitive to the level of carbon dioxide CO_2 in your blood. When the levels rise high enough, your body will breathe so that two things can happen – CO_2 is expired, and a new intake of oxygen can occur.

Many people over breathe, which generally results from mouth breathing. When we over breathe, we blow off too much CO_2, and there is no longer enough in the blood to stimulate the inspiratory control centre.

Mouth Breathing is also a common cause of asthma.

When you continually blow off too much CO_2 through the night, you lower blood pH, affecting energy levels. You wake tired.

It can be fixed using a breathing technique created early in the 20th century in Russia.

If you snore or have sleep apnoea and share a bed with another person, then it is your responsibility to fix the problem. The Buteyko Program will help you do that.

Buteyko Breathing Training

I was an asthmatic from the age of 5 and can remember the fear I felt during my first attack. My younger brother was worse and was clinically dead three times before the age of 2. But he survived, battling through life and the side effects of many different asthma medications.

The asthma I suffered was severe at times but perhaps never life-threatening. Although on occasions, it got scary when I could not breathe adequately to satisfy my need for oxygen. I was not too fond of the preventative medications because they left a constant residue on the back of my throat. So, I used Ventolin Inhalers more than I should, going through one every three weeks or so.

Training sessions were a killer. Every time I trained, the first 15 minutes were torture. I look back now and wonder how I ever did it. But I loved being fit so much that somehow, I pushed through it.

One day, at the age of 42, my wife's good friend Ursula came to visit. When I opened the door, I was gobsmacked at how alive and beautiful she looked. You see, Ursula was one of those asthmatics who ended up in hospital regularly. She was not a well girl.

But on this day, she looked vibrant and alive and the healthiest looking that I had ever seen her. "What has happened to you?" I exclaimed. "I don't have asthma anymore," she answered.

When I queried her, she told me she had done a Buteyko program, and she had cured her asthma. Now, I knew of Buteyko but had never bothered to give it a try. So now, I was motivated, and I took it on.

The Buteyko Breathing Program, a type of corrective physiotherapy, is the brainchild of a Ukrainian Medical Doctor named Dr. Konstantin Pavlovich Buteyko. He discovered the mouth breathing relationship to asthma in the 1950s and did many experiments, and finally devised a breathing program that alleviated the problem. You see, most asthmatics are mouth breathers. Often, this starts as a response to panic and anxiety. I know mine did. I struggled starting school and experienced a lot of anxiety, which led me to shallow mouth breathing.

So, at the age of 42, I finally decided to take the Buteyko Program seriously. It was one of the most challenging things I have ever done. It was tough work, especially in the first week. But I stuck at it. If Ursula could do it, then so could I. Within 2 weeks, the wheezing was gone, and I have not wheezed a breath since. Nearly 20 years on, I am no longer an asthmatic.

You can imagine my excitement when I heard that Buteyko also produces similar results with snoring and sleep apnoea and is also extremely helpful in reducing the symptoms of emphysema and pleurisy.

So, if you are an asthmatic, or if you suffer sleep apnoea or if your snoring is reducing the quality of your or your partner's sleep, Google Buteyko and find a practitioner in your area. They will get you on the road to excellent health and fantastic sleep.

Take Action – Get Results. Following is Sam's Story.

A few years ago, I arrived at a Local Government Office in Melbourne's outer South East region to deliver a Men's Health Seminar. Arriving early as I usually do, I mingled with the early starters and had a chat over a cup of tea.

A young man with a huge grin came up to me and said, "G'day mate. How are you doing?" I greeted him back with a smile, and he responded to the look on my face by saying, "You don't remember me, do you?" I admitted that I did not and asked when we had met.

He said he was not surprised I did not recognise him as he was 32kg lighter than last time. I laughed and breathed a sigh of relief. Then, he asked if I recalled the previous time that I had delivered a Men's Health Seminars at the same Municipality's other offices about 18 months before, and I said I did.

He introduced himself as Sam and said he had come to me after the seminar for a private chat and some guidance. Following is what happened when we had that chat.

He told me his life was a complete mess. He was married with two young kids, but at the age of 31, he was in a desperate place. He was significantly overweight, had no energy, was feeling depressed, and he had terrible sleep apnoea. He said his wife slept in another room, they fought often and had not been intimate for a long time. The pressure and stress in his home was almost intolerable and he was deeply frightened his wife would leave. He had reached rock bottom.

He asked if the Buteyko Breathing program I talked about would help him. I responded by saying that it was entirely up to him. If he were prepared to take it on, he would get results. Of course, I could not guarantee how good the results would be, but he would see improvements. So, he looked me in the eye and said he was going to give it a go.

So, here he was, standing in front of me, beaming. So, I had to ask what had transpired.

He said he made the call later that day and went to see a Buteyko Practitioner a couple of days later to start his training. He shared that it was highly challenging but remembered me warning him that it would be, but it would gradually get easier. So, he took it on. He said the sleep apnoea symptoms started to reduce after only a week. He began to sleep better and was waking with more energy.

He made a concentrated effort to drink more water and continued with his program. As the weeks passed, the sleep apnoea ceased, and the snoring also significantly reduced. He also noticed his weight beginning to drop.

At this point, he was feeling better about himself and was a lot brighter at home. He became less reactive to his wife, and things began to settle.

From this point, he decided to start exercising, joined the local gym, and focused on eating much better. As a result, his performance at work improved, and everything began to move in a good direction.

So now, here he was standing in front of me, beaming broadly and looking fabulous. He said that he and his wife were back in love, sleeping together and enjoying their life. He was the fittest he had ever been and had so far lost 32kg and felt he could lose a few more. He said he was happy, excited about life and always had energy to take his kids to the park after work and play with them.

He was trying to thank me, which is sweet, but I just wanted to thank him. He had taken responsibility, and he had taken action. The ripple effect was enormous. Several of his friends had become inspired and were also taking action on their own lives.

It was a happy moment.

Shift Work

Shift work is a fact of life for many. Some seem to handle it efficiently, and some struggle. Nurses and Doctors, Process Workers, Miners, Long Haul Drivers, Emergency Services, Law Enforcement, and many other workers have done it for years. It is part of the deal.

As economies expand and the world's populations grow, more and more is being demanded from more and more industries, driving a demand for around-the-clock production, which sets up the need for shifts.

Over recent years there has been an astounding amount of research into what is the best mix of work time versus time off, and what roster mix works best in terms of days on and days off. But, unfortunately, it seems there are still a variety of vastly conflicting opinions as to what works best.

However, I tend to feel this is probably the case because so many of the aspects of fatigue are not being addressed in most organisations, so no matter which roster or shift mix workers are engaged in, many still feel the effects of fatigue.

Perhaps fatigue has little, if anything, to do with rosters or shift make-up. Instead, maybe it is all about self-management.

My best advice to you to assist with surviving shift work is to follow these simple guidelines.

Stay well hydrated. It may be better to drink a little too much water as opposed to not enough. If the nightshift temperatures are cold, drink hot herbal teas, especially those that offer a little stimulation like peppermint, ginger and green teas. Avoid relaxing teas.

Keep yourself to a strict routine of sleep-wake. Then, follow the same routine, for retiring and rising times and mealtimes that you follow when working the day shift.

Make sure your environment is conducive to sleep if you are working at night and need to sleep during daylight hours.

Avoid heavy, stodgy food when working at night.

Avoid energy drinks and other stimulants. Keep your coffees down to 3 or less per day.

Shift work requires a strict discipline around times for going to bed and for waking up. Daytime sleep also requires a darkened sleep environment.

- You should map out how it works for you on Day shift and then simply apply this to night shift.
- EG: If you normally get up 2 hours before work, do the same. What time would that be?
- If you normally exercise after work, keep doing that.
- If you normally eat a meal 3 hours after finishing work, do that.
- If you normally attend to hobbies or watch TV after the meal, do that.
- Know what time you need to go to bed.
- Once you have a routine set, then stick to it. Make it a rigid plan that everyone in your home understands.
- Make your room as dark as can be. And, if getting up to go to the bathroom will expose you to light, get a potty and place it by your bed.

Choose to enjoy your work. Resisting your work will lead to a rapid onset of boredom and fatigue. If you choose to get interested and decide to gain some enjoyment and fulfilment from the experience, then you will not resist, and the fatigue will not come. A great way to do this is to get interested in how you can best do the job well and support others with whom you are working.

If your role requires that you sit still, for example operating machinery or a console, take time to get off your seat and move around at every opportunity. Stretch out a little and get your larger muscle groups doing a bit of work. Doing some free squats or even jumping around on the spot will help to invigorate the body and get blood flowing.

Have a "Wide Awake" attitude. If you walk in dragging your feet because "you have to work at night" you are already behind the eight ball. Turning up "bright eyed and bushy tailed" is a better plan.

Stimulants and Sleep

- Caffeine before bed may prevent sleep. Be careful of Chocolate for this reason.
- Alcohol before bed may negate your first REM Cycle.
- High Drama television and movies can be over stimulating.
- Arguments and highly stimulating Video Games are also over stimulating.

Curing Night Sweats

Some people find themselves sweating profusely during the night. I remember years ago talking to an old friend, Jerry Attaway who was the High Performance Manager at the San Francisco 49ers for over 20 years, right through the period when they won multiple Super Bowls. He told me about a young guy who had just come in for summer training and wanted to see what the coach thought of his diet. So, he laid it out.

- Breakfast: 8 egg omelette and a double protein shake.
- Mid-morning: Double Protein Shake
- Lunch: A Chicken, some salad and a Double Protein Shake
- Mid-afternoon: Double Protein Shake
- Dinner: 500 gram Steak and a Double Protein Shake
- Late evening: Double Protein Shake

Attaway looked at him, and in his typical dry tone said, "Man. Do you piss a lot?" The young man admitted he sweated so badly at night he had to change his sheets twice each night. This is the result of way too much protein in the diet. It is not necessary and can be fatally toxic.

Eating a huge serve of protein rich food in the evening can do this to you.

Night sweats can also be the result of poor body temperature regulation. This can be caused by either a lack of Omega 3 fatty acids, or a badly skewed balance of Omega 6 to Omega 3 fatty acids. If it is the first option for you, taking an Omega 3 supplement should correct your body's temperature problems.

If it is the latter, you might need to cut down your consumption of cheap vegetable oils and margarines.

If you are going to reach for an Omega 3 supplement, I prefer to recommend things like Chia Seed Oil (or regular consumption of Chia Seeds), Walnut Oil or Flax Oil. I am not a huge fan of harvesting fish stocks just so that you or I can get Omega 3. There are other more sustainable ways to do it.

Stop the Night Coughing

Coughing at night can really suck. It keeps you awake and possibly the family awake too. Cough suppressant medications sometimes work, but most often, they are ineffective.

Coughs are typically associated with a chest cold or a chest infection. Many years ago, I was amazed when told by my Chinese Physician that chest infections and the resultant coughing were caused by too much heat in the chest, which created dampness and provides an environment for infection. He told me that all I needed to do to stop the cough was get the heat out of my chest.

On that day, he showed me a little trick that I used on my kids for years and very occasionally on myself if I got sick. The way to get the heat out of your chest is down through your feet. First, make a paste mixing cayenne pepper and water, then rub it on the soles of your feet. Then put some socks on and go to bed. Within minutes, the heat in the chest is drawn toward your feet, the chest relaxes, and the coughing stops.

If you do not have any cayenne, you can apply Vicks vapour rub to the soles of your feet.

Over the years, I have discussed this method with many alternative medicine practitioners, and they all wink and smile and say something like, "Yes. An old therapy, but it works like a treat."

Cayenne Pepper is one of those things that is always handy to keep in your cupboard at home. It is also good for your blood.

What Do You Believe about Sleep?

Sometimes, your beliefs about sleep are your biggest problem. For example, when people ask me when I get up in the mornings and tell them 4:15, they often go into a reactive spasm. This is because they hold a belief that it is "too early". But that is only a belief. For me, it is a perfect time to do some preparation for the day, get out for a run, make a few calls overseas, and set myself up for a great day.

If you believe 9:00 pm is too early to go to bed, then that is what you will experience. If you believe 5:00 am is too early (whatever that means), waking at 5 am will be a significant struggle for you, and you will start your day in resistance. It is good to be aware of how your mind is viewing things.

Further, researchers revealed something remarkable about how people felt after a poor sleep. They showed that the person felt physically impaired, tired and lethargic, primarily because of their belief about a poor night sleep instead of the bad night's sleep itself.

Remember, even if you slept poorly, you have still been resting.

A Busy Mind

If your mind is busy, you might need an activity to get your attention off the incessant thoughts and get it out of your mind. Of course, playing Solitaire with an actual deck of cards is helpful. But there are many things you can do. Here are some:

- Doing a Jigsaw Puzzle
- Doing Sudoku Puzzles
- Reading
- Playing a musical instrument
- Drawing
- Writing a Gratitude list
- Hand writing a letter
- Working on a hobby. There are others...

Sleep Meditation

Meditation is an activity involving getting your attention under your own control. You know those times when your attention is basically everywhere, and you have lots of thoughts running around in your mind and your body cannot relax.

Focusing on a single thing is using your will to control what your attention is doing. If you persist, your attention will submit and come under the control of your will. The thinking will stop. This is the idea behind counting sheep. You keep counting them in your mind, using your will to direct your attention to the task, and all of a sudden, your attention submits and you doze off.

If you have real trouble with managing your attention, drop me an email. There is a fabulous course you can download that will take a couple of hours to do that will really help.

- Meditation is a good tool to quiet the mind before sleeping.
- Other activities that can quiet the mind include
- Jigsaw Puzzles
- Art Work
- Sitting Quietly outside (in the warmer months)

There are many sleep meditations on YouTube and there are also many sleep meditation apps available for smartphones.

Eating to Nourish

I do not wish to go into a huge explanation about food in this book. That may be another project for another day. But I will give you a couple of tips:

Eat Lightly.

In our world, we have too much food available. I have been to the camps. There is so much food. It is like Christmas Lunch at a smorgasbord restaurant. You must control yourself. Perhaps allow yourself one big food session per week. The rest of the time, eat lightly.

Hydrate.

You should be consuming enough water each day that you need to have a big urination every couple of hours, and that urination should be close to water colour. When you are well hydrated, you are less likely to over-eat.

Protein

Avoid too much heavy protein at night. Aim to eat more vegetables and salads at night. And avoid heavily fried foods. The high protein content in meats and the high omega 6 fatty acid content in frying oils, can leave you sweating profusely at night.

Eat Slowly.
Enjoy your food. Avoid shovelling it into yourself. The slower you eat, the less likely you are to over-eat.

Mornings.
Hydrate thoroughly at least 30 minutes before you eat. This will ensure you are well hydrated at the start of the day and it will help to prevent you over eating at breakfast.

A Perfect Time to Lose Some Weight and Get Fit

While you are staying in camp, you can find some people who train and join them. I always knew that if I wanted to be fitter and go faster, I had to train with people who were better than me.

When you are living in camp you have the perfect opportunity to:

- Follow a training program.
- Eat well.
- Stay off the alcohol.
- Study your health.
- Get plenty of sleep.

Chapter Summary

You should be in good health and in a reasonable state of fitness to take on FIFO work.

Understanding health gives you power.

Medicine divided the body into systems and then created specialists for each system. These became disconnected and confusion arose along with disease rates.

Healthcare costs are rising at a staggering rate.

The terrible state of health in Australia has overloaded our healthcare system. This was the reason for all the lockdowns when Covid-19 hit, to stop the system becoming overwhelmed.

We spend a huge amount of money treating preventable diseases, and we spend little on programs designed to prevent these diseases.

We eat badly, we do not exercise enough, we consume too much alcohol, some smoke and many do not handle their stress. This creates disease.

Degenerative diseases are lifestyle diseases. That is the bottom line.

Since the Second World War, the massive increase in processing of food, the use of chemicals, sugar consumption, high salt consumption and the instantaneous impact of fast food, has changed how we feed our bodies.

Good sleep is crucial to good health and wellbeing.

Wakefulness, Non-Rem Sleep and Deep REM Sleep. Optimising Deep REM Sleep is crucial.

Sleep-wake Cycles are a natural rhythm. Creating habits that support these rhythms leads to good sleep.

Alcohol, exposure to the blue-white light of devices, and stress can interfere with these sleep cycles.

Do the calculations to learn what time you should be preparing for sleep.

Create an ideal sleep environment – dark, cool, and quiet. Perhaps have some white noise like an app that can give you the sound of rain, surf, or running water.

Create clear agreements with your partner to keep your bedroom free of distress.

If you snore, or have sleep apnoea, deal with it.

If you work shift work, keep your routine for going to sleep the same. Keep meal routines the same also.

Stay very well hydrated at all times.

Avoid stimulants before sleep, especially energy drinks.

Enjoy your work. Resisting your work leads to stress, fatigue, and poor mental health.

If you have night sweats, supplement Omega-3. Chia Seed Oil is ideal.

Night-time coughing interrupts sleep and is often caused by heat and dampness in the lungs. Applying Vicks to the soles of your feet and putting socks on when you go to bed, should drag the heat out of your chest.

If you have a bad night sleep, remember you rested. Do not talk yourself into exhaustion.

If your mind is busy, take action. Engage in an activity that will get your attention out of your mind.

Assume some discipline over your eating. Eat clean, fresh foods.

Avoid too much protein before going to bed. A lighter meal is best.

Be sure to hydrate well. Avoid going to bed dehydrated.

Being in a camp is the perfect time to put some effort into losing some weight if you need to. Take the opportunity to get a food and exercise plan. Sleep will be a big part of your success.

Life Tips from This Chapter

It matters not how unhealthy or how unfit you are. You can start today, and you will improve.

If you have not had a check up for a while, I suggest visiting an Integrative Physician. The reason I suggest this is that a GP, if they discover any problem areas, will likely want to put you on medications. Perhaps you don't need that. You could just need some wise guidance into some lifestyle changes and an Integrative Physician offers this.

An Integrative Physician is a GP who has undergone extensive, additional training. You can find an Integrative Physician here https://www.aima.net.au/.

If you wish to improve your fitness there are several things you can do. Here are some examples:

1. Engage a Personal Trainer, ask them to get you started on a program and check in with them ever 2 to 4 weeks.
2. Attend a Yoga Class and develop a basic practice you can do whilst away.
3. Join a Martial Arts Club, train while at home and practice while away. Follow the guidance of your instructors.

Drink 1 litre of water for every 25kg of body weight per day. When you are out in the heat, drink enough so that you need to have a big urination at least every two hours, and when you do, your urine should be close to the color of water. In some circumstances this may see you consuming 10 to 15 litres of water in a day. If so, make sure you use an electrolyte replacement supplement.

Ask your Integrative Medicine Doctor, or a Naturopath, to help you put a plan in place to develop a strong immune system.

If you are consuming a lot of sugar, get support to handle it.

Make sure you are sleeping well. If you are not, take action. I suggest reaching to a sleep specialist. There are some wonderful professionals listed on my website. Details are in the back of this book.

If you snore, or have sleep apnea, do something about it. Contact a Buteyko Practitioner listed on my website and talk to them about it.

When working Shift Work, be deliberate about managing your existence. Getting lazy around this will create hardship.

Use the time you are away to discipline yourself and improve your health. Your biggest challenges may be over-eating and the wet mess. If you can master these, you can use your time in camp to become a better version of you.

Who is the Person that You Would Like to Be?

I have spoken a lot about finding purpose and creating better things in your life. It is the path to happiness.

Who do you want to become? When you sit quietly and contemplate, who is the person that you would like to become. Batman and Iron Man are taken. So, I ask you to take this seriously. How are your children or friends going to describe you when you are one day laid to rest?

Happiness Does Not Come to You

Happiness does not come to you from somewhere or something or someone. You can feel happy whilst enjoying an experience, but that will never be the source of your happiness.

If you try to make it so, you will spend all your money and time trying to re-create those experiences in which you felt happy.

Happiness comes from liking who you are and the contribution you make in the world. It is something you create by the way you live.

I want every person reading this book to be happy. That is not just for your sake, but for the sake of all the people you meet, especially children.

I believe that what we are happy, we spread good in the world. We lift other people's spirits, and we relieve suffering. And we are certainly not prone to conflict and war.

The Delusion of Happiness

Over the years, I have spoken to countless people looking forward to something, like buying a new car, a home, or even going on a trip. In many cases, these people were convinced that once they got there, they would be ecstatic and would no longer feel stressed, sad, depressed, or anxious. They would be happy.

In each case that I could follow up on, the happiness was brief and did not last.

There is an old story of a man who accidentally and unknowingly rubbed some pungent smelling cheese onto his top lip. The smell was awful. So, he left the room he was in and went to another room to escape the smell. But it was still there. So, he went to yet another room, and, you guessed it, the smell was still there.

All your unhappiness is like the cheese on the man's lip. You take it with you to every new experience. And whilst the new situation might have you forget it for a while, it is still there.

All of it is being created within you. So why would you not create something different?

Becoming a Better Version of You.

Are you using this experience working FIFO to help you become the person you want to be? Becoming the person you want to be is something that cannot be put off till later.

It does not work to say to yourself that "once things get better", I will work on becoming a better person. That attitude will keep you stuck on the unhappiness mouse wheel forever.

"We must all wage an intense, lifelong battle against the constant downward pull. If we relax, the bugs and weeds of negativity will move into the garden and take away everything of value." ~ Jim Rohn

Becoming a better human being can start right now. And please, take note of this. Becoming better does not mean "having to be perfect". It means making efforts each day to develop better habits and relinquish unhelpful patterns.

There are so many things you can do, simple things, that will help you grow and become better. Consider the following list of examples:

- Be more kind to others, especially strangers.
- Be helpful whenever you get the chance.
- Lift people up with encouragement.
- Avoid putting people down.
- Smile more.
- Be quiet and listen to people.
- Take a humble back seat in a group and enjoy others.

- Appreciate things. Not everything or everyone is going to be perfect. Appreciate that.
- Practice Gratitude daily.
- Eat better.
- Get some exercise.
- Get more sleep.
- Drink less alcohol.
- Take greater pride in your appearance.
- Do a favour for someone.
- Do random acts of anonymous kindness.
- Sponsor a kid in poverty.
- Visit a lonely person and take them for coffee.
- Ring someone you have wronged and apologise to them or send them a card.
- Organise a working bee to fix something in your neighbourhood that has been neglected.
- Pay for someone's coffee.
- Mow a neighbour's lawn.
- Read a Self-Development Book.
- Watch a Self-Development Video.
- Listen to an informative podcast.
- Write a letter to someone who is doing good work in the world, acknowledging them for their efforts.

There are so many things you can do. Share ideas around with your friends. Listen for what others are doing.

Please note that you will have days when you will be anything but the version of you that you wish to be. If that happens, get over it and double your efforts. It is ok. You are a human being, and you are learning something new.

How do You Imagine Yourself?

We all have a persistent image of ourselves in our minds. Often it is not great. We see negative parts of ourselves that have manifested over time, and we regret them. They stick there like an immovable label and dominate our view of ourselves.

I invite you to sit quietly for a moment and get honest with yourself about those private viewpoints you hold about yourself. The negative ones will come from somewhere. They are there because our actions were not great at one time or another, and we are deeply embarrassed about how we behaved or felt humiliated when we recall an event.

Here is the wake-up call. That is who you were being at that time. But it was not who you are. Remember, the Lakota Sioux Indians had a saying I mentioned a little way back. "You are who you are. You are not what you have done."

Now visualise yourself as you would like to be seen. What actions do you need to take daily to make that the permanent image of how you see yourself?

I have a sense that if you allow the negative image to remain, you will eventually re-create an event that will validate it. You do not want to do that.

Things Take Time: Patience, My friend.
When you are setting out to work on yourself and your life, some things you want seem too far off. For example, you might want to learn to play the guitar. However, you know it might take a few years, so you feel discouraged before you even start.

But what would you be doing now if you had started three years ago?

I have a close friend who was looking for a new sport at age 19. She chose Karate. By the time she was 30, she had won 6 world heavyweight titles. Her skills took her forward to become a world champion in another sport and eventually become a personal bodyguard for an Academy Award-winning actor. Some would have said that 19 is too old to start as a novice in Karate.

It does not matter how long something will take. An old saying tells us, "The Journey is the Destination". It is who you become whilst working on getting better at your craft that is often most important.

If there is something you want to do, start. If you do not know how to do it, find a teacher. Check YouTube.

The Thing I have Learned About Men.

I have watched, studied, talked to people, and done courses. I have sat through classes with so-called gurus who believe they have the answers for men.

This includes programs based on American Indians to programs that followed "The Iliad". Yet, all the while, I felt that something was missing.

One program touched on Archetypes of Men, the main ones being The King, The warrior, The Artist and The Lover. This one made some sense until further, more detailed studies of Archetypes left this one a little less appealing.

In recent times whilst speaking to groups on sites, talking to men across Australia and observing more, I got to feel some interesting things.

Some men are incredible artists. I watch in awe at the artistic talents of so many artists, actors, filmmakers, musicians, and comedians.

Others are intellectuals, and they use their intellect to invent, guide, manage, and streamline things.

Then there are the men who like to build things.

I have a strong sense there is a little of the latter in all men. When I contemplate history, as people moved about or as people moved into new lands, the men assumed the roles of home builder and maintainer, water engineer, farmer, animal wrangler, weapon builder and hunter.

His daily life involved using his problem-solving skills and physical strength to overcome challenges and obstacles and keep life moving for his family and community.

His family and community needed him to do these things. And, on a daily or weekly basis, as the man achieved these things, as he overcame challenges, his sense of value, self-esteem and self-worth grew. With that came happiness and contentment. And, as time passed, he handed the skills on to his sons.

When I look around at life today, I ask myself where most men get access to the opportunity to do these things, overcome challenges with their problem-solving skills and physical strength?

For many, the opportunity does not exist. Life is too well sorted, and many men never get to do anything that leaves them feeling good about themselves. They do not ever get to do anything that tells them they are valuable in their community and that their contribution is needed and appreciated.

They never get to "show up" as a man. Hence, many find themselves doing stupid things like demonstrating how much they can drink or how they can fight, measuring themselves against more obscure and less helpful yardsticks of masculinity.

But all is not lost. I feel that men can find this fulfilment quite easily and quickly. There are so many areas in the world in which they are needed right now.

Consider the following:

- Getting together to find a family where there may be a single parent situation, where poverty is close at hand, and where the home needs repair. Work together as a team to repair that house and give that struggling family a safe place to live.
- Find the elderly and lonely people in the neighbourhood and get them involved in the community, perhaps the local football club. Take them to training nights and to games. Find out how they would like to contribute.
- Bring back working bees in the community, at schools and around public areas to repair something that is failing, or to build something that is needed.
- Get involved in youth programs and take young people out and teach them how to fish, or how to repair a car.

- If you are a mechanic or car enthusiast and love working on cars, find out from a local youth program if there are two or three teenagers who love cars. Go buy a car that is all but dead, and work with them to restore it and bring it back to life. If you repeat over time with two or three cars, these young people can have their first car. And they will know how to keep it going.
- If you are a lover of growing things, lobby your council to allow you to use some public land to plant organic vegetables and invite people in the community to participate.
- I could write 100 or more of these suggestions, but I'd prefer you reach into your own imagination and discover your original ideas and your inspiration.

You can create great things. You can go to bed every night feeling so good about who you are and how you conduct your life. But you must take the first step.

Keep Evolving

We all must keep evolving. As many great teachers continue to tell us, it is the path of life and the only authentic way to find happiness.

When you take on new challenges that leave you feeling like a novice, you are forcing yourself to overcome fear, self-doubt, concern, embarrassment, and failure to get to your goal. These are things that give you the impetus for growth.

You do not have to be The Man to be A Man!

Following is an article I wrote in 2019. I feel it fits here.

A few days ago, I was having a conversation with a café owner. He talked about men in their 50's who had left their marriages and started a new life with a much younger woman.

He was saying, "They all look the same, they say the same things, and their parting statements to their wives as they left was pretty much the same. And now they find themselves in a similar situation, none of them is happy, and they are stuck with younger families".

At first, I thought, "Wow! That is a pretty big generalisation." Maybe it is true. I guess I have not hung out with enough men in that position to know. But it left me contemplating and wondering what it is all about.

As I ran this morning, something landed for me. Back when I was in my mid 30's, I used to have this feeling that nagged at me. "When am I going to stop feeling like an overgrown teenager and start feeling like a Man?" At the time, my first marriage was all but over, and I was CEO of a relatively new business struggling to make its way in the world. Brand new markets needed to be forged, and our potential customers were not really in a place where they felt a need for our product.

At the time, I was working crazy hours, struggling financially after being "crunched" by sky-high interest rates from the 1989 recession, trying to be a good Dad and often in desperation trying to get my staff paid. As a result, I was taking shortcuts, bullshitting a lot and hoping it would all get better.

Two things happened around that time. First, I started reading Self Development Books, and second, one of my employees, a brilliant and gentle guy, sat me down and told me some things I needed to hear. It was excruciatingly uncomfortable and humiliating, but it was one of the kindest things anyone had ever done for me.

Along the way, as I read, explored and contemplated my life, I realised that feeling like I had made it as a man wasn't something that magically happens one day. Instead, it was a decision I needed to make, to finally decide to leave my adolescence behind and be a man.

Until then, I have a sense I was running off my age-old impressions of movie heroes, sporting superstars and iconic men in my society and in my life, whom I looked up to as being men who were more manly than others. These men seemed to have a dominant presence in life, an aura of power and significance. So I guess that, in my mind, you were not a man until you were that.

But I realised something straightforward. You do not have to be "The Man" to become "A Man". It set me free, and I felt I could relax and just be my version of a man, my maturity and my masculinity.

So, I have a sense that some males aged 40 to 60 might still be trapped in this misunderstanding about their manhood. I imagine the same probably happens for women. I have a sense it has very little to do with gender and more about simply owning who we are and taking our place in the world.

When I finally made that decision, I could more easily feel responsible and take greater responsibility. I also realised that the way I looked at life and events changed.

Now, I am over 60, and I feel that it is still a daily decision to be a responsible adult male in the world. I train a lot and enjoy feeling as youthful as I can. But my maturity, wisdom, care, and leadership are perhaps more important to those around me in the world.

I now understand why Clint Eastwood makes different movies these days, perhaps starting with "The Unforgiven" through to The Mule. He portrays men, not as demigods like The Outlaw Josey Wales or Dirty Harry Callaghan but as vulnerable and often damaged men seeking to find their place in the world. He perhaps realised that trying to be "Dirty Harry" has taken many good men down some dark allies.

It is such an exciting perspective. You do not have to be "The Man" to become "A Man"!

Chapter Summary

Who do you want to be? What type of person do you want to be? Are you moving in the direction of becoming that person or away from it?

Happiness does not come from somewhere outside of you. It is created by you, within you. It may well come from you learning to like who you are.

Happy people spread goodness in the world and lift the spirits of others.

Achieving milestones and acquiring things like new cars and homes can be tremendous. But they are no guarantee of happiness.

Some people become someone they do not like to gain these things.

Are you using this experience of working FIFO to become a better version of yourself?

"Once things get better" is delusional. You can start now.

There are many simple steps you can take to become a better human being.

You will have bad days. But those days are just "bad days", not your life story.

How do you view yourself in your mind? Are you being kind to yourself?

"You are who you are. You are not what you have done." Lakota Sioux Indians

Who do you want to be able to see yourself as being? What actions do you need to take to get to that place?

It is essential to be patient with yourself.

It is never too late to start developing a new skill or growing yourself to be better.

The "Journey is the Destination". When you set a new goal, you are forced to grow.

YouTube has thousands of wonderful teachers sharing their craft. Take a look.

All people like to achieve things. It seems one of the age-old roles of men was to overcome problems to ensure the needs of his community were met.

In modern life, there is not much of that for men to do. You cannot even jump start a car anymore.

The problems now exist in people's minds. So helping people find their way through "stinking thinking" is needed right across society today.

Take responsibility for your own thinking. Then help others take responsibility for theirs.

Show up for the kids who do not have a Dad to support them.

Get your mates together and do some repairs on the home of a poverty-stricken family.

Become a friend to an older adult. Take them for a walk, for a coffee, for a beer, or to the local footy club. Talk with them. Introduce them to people.

Get involved in things that support disaffected youth. For example, if you are a fisherman, teach a lost young man to fish.

There are so many things you can do. Help someone else.

Keep evolving. Never miss a chance to grow a little.

Remember, all that macho stuff you might have grown up on is false.

You do not have to be "The Man" to be "A Man."

Life Tips from This Chapter

Remember this basic rule of life. Happiness comes from the contributions you make to the lives of others. It never comes from the things you receive. Doing things in the world that benefit others in some way will always leave you feeling good about yourself.

Buying an expensive car, whilst fun to drive, may get you some attention, or may have you feeling more successful or important, but you will only feel good about yourself when you are in the car.

I recommend reading books that guide and inspire you. You can either buy the book, download the eBook, or download the talking book. All are ok. I recommend the following:

- "A Fortunate Life" by A B Facey
- "The Four Agreements" by Don Miguel Ruiz
- "The Road Less Travelled" by M. Scott Peck
- "Healing Lives", By Sue Williams
- "Rich Dad, Poor Dad" by Robert Kyosaki
- "The Avatar Path: The Way We Came." By Harry Palmer
- "The Art of Happiness", By His Holiness, The Dalai Lama
- "The Seven Habits of Highly Effective People", By Stephen Covey
- "From Death Camp to Existentialism", By Viktor Frankl
- "Think and Grow Rich", By Socho Aur Amir Bano
- "How to Win Friends and Influence People", By Dale Carnegie
- "Who Moved My Cheese", By Spencer Johnston
- "7 Strategies for Wealth and Happiness", By James Rohn

Write an Affirmation about who you want to become. Write it down and read it every day. Start it out with "I am…".

Invite your partner to take the self-improvement journey with you.

Take time to learn more about practicing virtues and living a virtuous life. Consider things like: Kindness, Compassion, Mercy, Forgiveness, Encouragement, Acknowledgement, Gratitude, Selfless Service, Empathy, Acceptance, Appreciation, Respect, Honesty, Truth, Humility, Support and so many others. Start with being kind to yourself.

Try some of the suggestions on page 230.

Do what you can do to support the women in your workforce and in your community. Don't stand for sexism, inequality, or abuse. Do what you can to make it safe for all women to live a full and rewarding life.

Find something that you can do in your community, something that allows you to add value. It may be taking up a role with a community sports club or helping out with a community initiative. When you find that thing, make a commitment to it for the next year and see what you can achieve.

When you walk out your door each day, take a moment to set yourself. Take a moment to feel what it will feel like today to be:

- Humble
- Kind
- Compassionate
- Caring
- And to have Guardianship for all that is around you.

Learning to Meditate

There is nothing mysterious about meditation. It is a practice in disciplining your mind.

Most people have tens of thousands of thoughts run through their mind each day. Some of those thoughts fly by and others stick, and we ruminate on them.

When we are consumed with thinking, not much of our attention is directed out into the world. On a dangerous work site, being consumed with thinking places you in danger, as you may not notice things you should.

At night, being consumed with thinking, especially stressful thought, can interfere with sleep and cause you to be tired when it is time to get out of bed and start your day.

Thoughts come and go. That is what they do. They may be triggered by unresolved issues, fears, worries or desires. They may pop up in response to something you see or hear in your environment. They may be completely random.

Stressful thoughts can trigger responses in your body. Those responses can include anxiety symptoms, which are never comfortable.

The trick to gaining control over your thinking is learning to discipline your mind. As you become better at doing so, your mind is less likely to respond automatically, and you will be more able to keep your attention where you want it to be.

As you build your skill in disciplining your mind, you will find yourself becoming more peaceful and more aware. It can lead you to a state of mindfulness that will improve your safety, your experience of life and your inner peace.

There Are Many Techniques

Meditation has many techniques. Some are done with eyes open and others with eyes closed. Some use a mantra (a word or a phrase that you repeat over and over). Others involve looking at an object or picture. Some are done sitting while others are done standing up and walking around. Some involve placing all your attention on your breath. Here are some basic descriptions.

Basic Seated Meditation – Time 5 minutes up to an hour.
Sit quietly in a comfortable position, in a chair, on the floor or on a bed. Make sure you are upright, and your back is straight. Breathe slow and deep, in through your nose, and out through your mouth. Close your eyes and place all your attention on a single thing. It might be your breathing, or an image of something in your mind, or a short phrase you enjoy. As you sit there, focusing your attention, notice any thoughts that come into your mind. Simply acknowledge them and then let them go by. If your mind gets caught up and you get lost in thought for a bit, just bring it back and focus again. Meditation is a practice. It has never been about doing it perfectly.

Additional Tip: Sometimes I will use this meditation but will turn on some music I love. It needs to be a full sound with complexities. I often use Pink Floyd or Classical Music. I take myself inside the music and explore all the sounds, seeking out the more subtle changes and variations. It is a different way to experience your favourite music. But all the time, I am directing my attention.

Note: It may be an idea to set a soft alarm to let you know when your time is up. As your practice grows, you may find time passes quickly.

Open Eyes Variation
This is much the same as the seated meditation described earlier, but in this case, you open your eyes and look at something. It could be a candle flame, or a beautiful picture. Intensify your gaze as you look, seeing if you can place more and more of your attention on the thing you are looking at, to discover more about it. You are strengthening your ability to direct your attention. If thoughts come in, treat them as I described in the basic seated meditation.

Tibetan Walking Meditation
This meditation requires you to go outside and move, taking small and big steps, forward, sideways, or backwards, stepping slowly and carefully, all the while, seeking to place your foot down without making a sound.

Imagine a martial artist walking silently through an enemy camp. It is active and requires a great deal of focused attention.

A Walk in Awe

Best done out in nature, this meditation requires you to go walking and choose to be in a state of complete awe at the wonder and beauty of everything around you. Flowing your attention further and further out into the world, see if you can notice more and more subtleties. Be in awe of the wonder and beauty of mother nature.

Hobbies and Other Activities

By now, you may have realised that some of your favourite activities are meditative. Anything that has you directing your attention toward a single point can be meditative. For some it is working with wood, or fishing, working in the garden or painting. Whatever works well for you is ok.

Jigsaw puzzles can be a brilliant meditation as you require all your attention to find the pieces you seek.

Other Guidance

There are countless meditation Apps in the App Stores. Download some and try them out.

My good friend Neal Hoptman is also a wonderful Meditation Teacher. Neal has been a Yogi for over 40 years and travels the world teaching others about Wellness, Yoga and Meditation. You can visit his website at https://www.virtualhealthresort.com/. Go to the resources section on "Experiencing a Peaceful Mind" where you can access comprehensive guidance and information about meditation.

Further, my good friend Tami Roos, is a Psychology PhD and specialises in Meditation. She has been teaching across the world for years and in recent times, has supported her husband Paul's Football Coaching by teaching the players at the Sydney Swans and Melbourne how to meditate and how to make regular meditation practice a part of their lives.

You can learn more from Tami at https://tamiroos.com/.

In it for the Long Haul.

You should sit in meditation for 20 minutes per day unless you do not have time. Then you should do 60 minutes."

Zen Buddhist Saying

"Don't just do something. Sit there!"

Osho

Chapter Summary

A busy mind is common in the 21st century. But you do not have to be at the effect of it.

Meditation is a practice.

Try to make time daily to do a meditation.

It is a practice of learning to discipline your attention and gain control over your mind.

Meditation can be done in a variety of ways.

Choose a technique that feels right for you and begin your practice.

Many hobbies are meditative in their nature.

You can download Apps to help you with your meditation.

Taking a Bigger Picture View of Life

Sometimes we can get very lost in our own world. So often, it can seem that our struggles are so different to everyone else's, perhaps even more significant. Nobody could possibly understand. Right?

Then there are times when lost in our world means that everything is going so well and we feel so good about it that we start to feel like a bit of an expert, pretty unique and important. But, whether positive or negative, the outcome is still the same, and we get caught up in it.

Of course, none of that is terrible, but it is interesting to observe.

We can get so lost in our concerns that we forget there are others. We also forget that others may need our help and support. We are all capable human beings, and many of us could give more than we do.

What does ANZAC Day mean to you?

I have rarely missed an Anzac Day dawn service since I was a kid. But, growing up in Miles in Queensland, from the age of 7, I became acutely aware of Anzac Day and the sacrifice the diggers made. Miles is a small town, so the entire community stopped for the Anzac Day parade. The Dawn Service was held across the street from our Pub in Memorial Park, where an old World War 1 cannon stood as a solemn reminder and curiosity for kids.

The stories always touched me. The question I always ask myself is, "Would I be prepared to do that for my country?" Never yet have I been able to say "Yes" to myself honestly. The courage of those young men was extraordinary.

In 1982 when Great Britain decided to go to war with Argentina over the Falkland Islands, I was anxious that I would be called up. As a fit and athletic 22-year-old Surf Lifesaver, I could have been in line for a call if Australia sent troops to support England. It got to the point where I loathed the sound of the 3XY News music and had to stop using the radio for a morning alarm. The thought of going to war scared the hell out of me.

Of course, we can get caught up in arguments about how wrong war is. But that is a waste of effort because the reality is that those young men left Australia, knowing full well they may never come back, and walked headlong, chest out, into an earthly form of hell. They did it because they cared more for others than for themselves.

I ask groups of men if they take time to recognise Anzac Day and attend services. Many do. When I ask what they are observing, many talk about the courage and the sacrifice, the Anzac Spirit.

The Anzac Spirit

The Anzac Spirit is something that Australians revere. What is it? I would define it as "being willing to gladly give of oneself so that one's family, community and greater society may be safe, and have the freedom to live their lives".

It is a noble intention. But, imagine what would happen to a society if every person followed that intention as their fundamental ethic for life.

I guess the opposite of the Anzac Spirit is selfishness. And I feel that over the past 50 years, selfishness has crept in more deeply each year to the heart of our culture. We have moved from "in it together" more toward "everyone for themselves".

Covid-19 seemed to shine a very bright light on this reality. First, I was amazed and encouraged by how many people decided to follow our leaders and comply with the restrictions. Then some got lost in themselves and either wanted to rebel or horde essential goods at the supermarkets. It was profound to see. But it went further, as those who did choose to comply seemed to maintain a sense of humour and did not appear to get caught up in what the "me me me" crowd were doing.

These events told me that when times get tough and threats appear, the essential quality of the Anzac is still very much alive in most Australians. So, my question is, "How do we get better at having attention on the welfare of others when there is no danger or imminent threat?"

Old People Who Grow Fruit Trees

Do you ever wonder about older people who plant fruit trees? It will take years for that tree to bear fruit. The tree will not bear fruit till long after their life is over. Yet, they still plant that tree with love and care.

It is a profound act of service. These people live their life with future generations in mind. Working and toiling in the soil so that people they will never meet can enjoy the fruits of their labour.

Imagine if the whole world, companies too, put their attention on how they impact future generations. Imagine if everyone took a moment in their daily lives and asked themselves, "Am I helping make things better in the world today, or am I creating a problem?"

I am sure there have been many days when I have taken from the world, consumed more than my share, or even created problems in the world. None of this is about becoming a perfect human being, just a better human being.

When you are out on-site, what can you do to make life better for someone else? First, of course, you must figure that out for yourself. But imagine what you could do.

Who Did Build those Roads?

When I fly across Australia, I look down and see roads that stretch right across the continent. Some have been there for many decades, connecting cities and towns and connecting the inland to coastal ports.

It is as if they are the vital arteries of the landscape, allowing humans to live and thrive in this harsh land.

But how did they get there? They were built during a time before we had ever heard of FIFO, built by men who left their homes a week or so after Christmas and returned more than 11 months later. These were the hardy souls who forged the fundamental infrastructure of the land, the infrastructure that allowed towns and cities to grow.

They constructed roads, bridges, laid railway tracks and installed telegraph lines. Eventually, they established power lines. These incredible human beings worked in service to a future they would never see, laying the foundations for a new and exciting nation. They had the Anzac Spirit. They gave so that others may live.

Your Part in it

When you work in mines, or oil and gas, or in a service that supports these, you are playing your part in the delivery of vital resources that will build cities, infrastructure, machinery, and all manner of goods that will contribute to the lives of many.

The world uses mineral resources to create and grow, and your work is the starting point. So I invite you to celebrate your role in the building of the future.

Service to the Betterment of Humanity

Watch a small child when they do something nice for someone else. Perhaps they make a piece of toast and serve it to mum in bed. When they deliver their gift, they feel so good about themselves. It is human nature to do so.

Taking part in activities that reduce suffering or improve someone's quality of life is time well spent.

Many years ago, my sister rang and asked if I minded too much if she did not buy me a Christmas present that year. I told her I was not fussed, asked whether she might be short of money, which she was not, and told her I would still be getting her one.

On Christmas day, she was light and happy. When I asked what was going on, she declined to give me any data, but I knew she had been up to something.

Many years later, I begged her to tell me what she had done that Christmas. "Oh, that!" she said. "I have never told anyone about that."

She continued, "There is a huge gaming venue in my area, and I knew there would be families with no money for Christmas. So, I visited the local Priest to ask if he knew of any, and he told me there were five families in terrible financial trouble due to poker machines. So, I purchased five large Wicca baskets and five of everything that would make a good Christmas like Hams, Turkeys, Christmas cake, plum puddings, custard, summer fruits, shortbread, drinks, Christmas stockings etc. I packed them up on Christmas Eve, wrapped them in green and red cellophane, and put an anonymous Christmas Card on top. Then, late that night, the Priest helped me quietly place them on the front doorsteps of those homes."

I sat there stunned and eventually asked how she felt about it now, and she replied, "Every time I remember it, I get a bit of a thrill and a flood of good feelings".

That is how my sister rolls. And it is probably the quality that took her to the pinnacle of her profession, never doing it for the money but always working to make things better.

A Collective Effort

In 2019 I was invited to deliver some seminars for a national company that tends to experience a lot of union tension and sometimes crippling disputes. I was invited to present on Physical Wellness at two of their busiest sites and was invited back to present on Care and Resilience.

The sessions were terrific. The connection I was able to create with the workforce was deep and genuine. I realised that this was a group of predominantly men who had good hearts but perhaps did not value themselves enough. I often find this. During my talk, I helped them feel more of their lives and the possibilities close at hand.

The session struck such a chord on one of the sites that many men sat quietly with watery eyes and tears rolling down their cheeks. It was beautiful. The manager said to me, "If I had not seen this, I would never have believed it".

Following the sessions, I wrote a recommendation to the company to invite the workforce to establish their own charitable foundation. I could feel that if these men came together as a group to support an effort that did some good in the world, perhaps relieve some suffering, workplace culture would improve. I suspect they would become much more content, productive, and less open to manipulation by an often militant union.

I suggested the company provide the support to establish the foundation structure and allow the workers to choose the foundation's purpose. Deep in my heart, I could feel that these men would thrive with such an addition to their careers. Moreover, their efforts would be voluntary, and they could contribute as much as they wanted.

For whatever reason, nothing ever came of it. Then, at the worst time ever, the workforce went on strike. The strike action was significant and highly disruptive. And the company personnel were back to doing what they obviously must love, battling the union.

Aligning yourself with a group of people to contribute to a valuable and worthwhile cause is powerful. It brings new incentives and motivation into your life. You feel part of something bigger than yourself. It is extraordinary. That is why service groups like Rotary and Lions are so successful.

Going to bed at night feeling good about who you are

If you would like to know the secret to great sleep, it is simple. Just live a life that allows you to go to bed at night feeling deeply content with who you are as a person.

When we live a life that creates conflict, selfishness, mistrust, anger, and resentment, we are left with a mind that wants to justify itself whilst at the same time reminding itself of how bad it is. It is spiralling down to the gates of hell and can often only be stopped by sedatives, alcohol, or some other drug.

Sleep is not an easy escape from that kind of mental noise.

When we live a selfish life, seeking to gain personal advantage, often creating conflict with others, we are degrading ourselves and our lives. Whilst our minds seek to convince us we are right and entitled, we have a moral code that knows what is right and what is not. We cannot escape that knowing. The result is self-loathing, which is often followed by more degrading behaviour.

Often, when we have behaved this way and wake up to it, we face a temptation to slip into regret. None of this helps. The best way to fix the problem is to start giving. Give kindness, support, service, empathy, care, and encouragement to others. Your efforts will repay a karmic debt, and peace will soon return.

Here is a simple reason to take a bigger picture view of life. The more goodness you put into the world, the more people will feel lifted by you. They, too, will put goodness out into the world. These actions have a magnifying effect. It will not be long before you or someone close to you is impacted by the virtuous actions of another person.

Chapter Summary

A common trap is to get lost in the struggles of your mind. As a result, you end with all your attention on yourself and can become consumed and self-absorbed.

And then sometimes you can get a little drunk on your own fumes when things seem to be going well.

You forget about others. You forget that others could benefit from our help.

ANZAC Day is a special time on the Australian and New Zealand Calendar. It is a time for reflection, gratitude, and awareness of the horrors of stupidity and conflict.

What does ANZAC Day mean to you? What do you celebrate? What is the ANZAC Spirit?

Have you ever been to war? Have you ever contemplated what you would do if you were compelled to go to war? How would you handle it? Honestly!

The ANZAC Spirit: "being willing to gladly give of oneself so that one's family, community and greater society may be safe, and have the freedom to live their lives".

The opposite of the ANZAC Spirit is probably selfishness. Unfortunately, selfishness has crept into the Australian psyche over the past 50 years at an alarming rate.

During the Covid-19 Pandemic, this selfishness seemed to subside as people sought to do the right thing and work together to prevent the spread of the virus. Nevertheless, a few were consumed by self-importance, and they stood out.

It seems that when times get tough and threats appear, or when disaster strikes, the ANZAC Spirit reveals itself.

How do we get better at having attention on the welfare of others when there is no danger or imminent threat?

Why do older adults grow fruit trees they know they will never see bear fruit?

Do you live your life with future generations in mind? Do you take from the world more than you give?

What can you do today to make life better for someone else?

When you look at the profound infrastructure that stretches across this wild country, much of it has been there for decades. Do you ever wonder how it got there?

My best guess is that the ANZAC Spirit made it possible and turned it into a reality.

Are you clear on your connection to how your daily efforts benefit the lives of others?

Taking part in activities that reduce suffering or improve someone's quality of life is time well spent.

Aligning yourself with a group of people to contribute to a valuable and worthwhile cause is powerful. It brings new incentives and motivation into your life.

When you go to bed feeling good about who you are, you sleep peacefully.

A mind that needs to justify its actions through the day cannot rest. Finding sleep is challenging.

When you are selfish, you are likely to act in ways that will have you degrading yourself.

Give kindness, support, service, empathy, care, and encouragement to others. Your efforts will repay a karmic debt, and peace will soon return.

The more goodness you put into the world, the more people will feel lifted by you. They, too, will put goodness out into the world. These actions have a magnifying effect. It will not be long before you or someone close to you is impacted by the virtuous actions of another person.

Life Tips from This Chapter

Who do you want to be? What sort of person do you want others to see you as being? When this is clear to you, what can you do each day to move closer to being that person?

What is your vision for Australia? How can you help our country move in that direction?

Contemplate The ANZACS and the Anzac Spirit. How can you bring that more into your life? How can you make your life mean more toward the betterment of circumstances for others?

What will your legacy be? What will you leave behind when you pass that your community will value?

How can you help your friends and colleagues to show up in the world and become better, contributing citizens?

Look around the community and see what is needed. Then ask yourself what skill you have and where you can apply them to something that is needed in the community.

Choose to be kind and understanding. Give people the space they need for their journey. But always, when needed, step up and protect those who are vulnerable or in difficulty.

Join a group in the world who are doing good work. The Male Hug is wonderful. https://themalehug.com.au/

Revisiting Your Goals

Now that you have completed the book, it could be a great time to revisit your goals. Perhaps you did not have goals in the first place.

It is never too late to set a goal and set about working toward it.

When you set a worthwhile goal that inspires you, it challenges you to grow. Every great teacher will tell you that you need to become better if you want a better life. Unfortunately, a better life will rarely be delivered to you.

The world is littered with broke lottery winners.

The purpose of this book is not to become a Goal Setting Tool. However, there are many out there in the world. There are books available, and there are programs on YouTube.

I will give you one piece of advice, though. Achieving a goal is hard work. You must overcome your laziness daily. You must be able to push through when you do not feel like it.

So my advice to you is to read good books that help you grow and get better. There are thousands of books out there in the world written by good people who want to help others.

Some are written by would-be gurus who want to show you how much they know.

There are videos on YouTube that you can watch or listen to that provide profound guidance. If you go to my YouTube Channel, you will find some great videos there. There are Self Development videos on my channel, and Goal Setting and other videos designed to help you.

https://www.youtube.com/channel/WideAwakeWellness

Becoming a Helper

Would you like to learn more about these areas? Would you like to gain greater skills so that you can achieve more as a person, and be able to help more people?

Are you curious about the grand possibilities of life?

If you would like to learn more about what is possible, email me at jt@wideawakewellness.com.au and I will direct you to some of the training I have done over time. This is training that helps you move well beyond your limits, transcend your mind and to be able to live in your heart.

When you get to that place, you will intuitively know how you can help others in your own unique way.

Acknowledgements

Back in 1980, whilst working at The Golden Bowl, Melbourne's first ever multi facility indoor sports centres, as a gym instructor, I met Chris Jones.

Chris, originally from Liverpool, and an accomplished drummer, basketballer, and rugby union player, had come to Melbourne from Oregon to take over as Health Director "The Bowl" and The Ultimate Sporting Club, Australia's first 5 Star, exclusive, Health and Fitness Club.

I didn't know what to think of Chris at first. He was a big man with a stern persona. Over the next few years, working under him, I learned everything I needed to get started in an exciting career. His profound intellect, coupled with deep kindness and patience, got in behind my best efforts to make something of myself.

As a speaker, he taught me how to teach people. And, when I asked him to edit a Sports Trainers Handbook I had been commissioned to write, he delivered profound lessons. My writing had never been good. In fact, it was terrible. Sitting with me patiently for three hours, quizzing me and urging me to dig deep, it landed. I understood how to write.

He did what no schoolteacher had time to do, and what great mentors always do. He gave me, time, care, and patience.

So, thank you Chris Jones. You are one in a million my friend, and the world is much better place because of your contributions.

In 2005, I walked into a course room in a large hotel on The Gold Coast, to being my journey through The Avatar Course, authored and originated by Harry Palmer. On the morning of the 9th Day I experienced a powerful awakening, a deep separation between my essential being and my mind. If moved on to complete all of Harry's Courses, and taught Avatar for years. I live with a deeply quiet mind, profoundly expanded awareness and moment-to-moment access to my intuition. I am forever grateful for this most powerful gift.

About The Author

I was born on a Cattle Station about 50km from Roma in Queensland, Australia, in 1960. In 1963, we moved to a Dairy Farm outside Toowoomba, and then in 1967 to The Windsor Hotel in Miles. In 1970, with 8 kids in tow, my parents sold up, headed for Melbourne, and took over the Morning Star Hotel in Hoddle Street Abbotsford, a tough inner Melbourne suburb and a melting pot of new immigration.

Over the next 6 years, I learned many great lessons. First, I had to learn how to be part of what was going on but stay out of trouble. Three years of Christian Brothers education toughened me up. I spent my final three years at Marcellin College, a wonderful school where I realise that I could create a great life if I so desired.

Four years studying Physical Education followed. I became heavily involved in Surf Lifesaving at Jan Juc and played a lot of Football. In 1983 as an Amateur, I represented Victoria and was the lone emergency for the All-Australian Amateur Team.

My footy success was not based on Natural Talent but a love of training. I planned my training and worked hard. The older blokes at Marcellin Old Boys used to call me SOS, which years later I learned stood for Son of Spartacus.

I quit playing at 24 because I wanted to study more and work in High Performance Roles in the then VFL. I enrolled in a Masters Program at Victoria University and in 1986 started as Head of Conditioning for Richmond Football Club.

When I was 21, I helped my best mate develop Australia's first Fitness Leadership Course. It was his idea and his baby, to help train aerobics instructors. A few years later, I developed a course for Gym Instructors. I realised then that I wanted to teach people about Health, Fitness and living an energetic life. I wanted people to Thrive.

Over the years between 1986 and 1999, I worked in several VFL/AFL Clubs and, also, delivered a lot of seminars in companies on Fitness, Nutrition, Disease Prevention, Stress Management and Work Life Balance.

I stepped away from Sports Conditioning at the end of 1999 as I wanted to go full time in Workplace Wellbeing Education.

Over the years, I have continued to study and learn. I have worked with people of diverse talents including Yogis, Qi Gong Masters, Doctors, Naturopaths, Osteopaths, Chinese Physicians, Ayurvedic Physicians, Meditation Teachers, Artists, Musicians, Spiritualists and would be gurus. Since 2005, I have studied Human Consciousness extensively using The Avatar Course Materials developed by Harry Palmer.

All the while I have sought how I can inspire people, educate them and give them the knowledge and the impetus to act. Supporting another human to become personally responsible for their life is perhaps one of the greatest gifts we can give. A few years ago, I was finally able to articulate my mission.

To touch the lives of thousands of Families, by providing exceptional and helpful education, guidance, and inspiration to workers, so that they may be safer and more productive at work and more engaged, happy and content at home, and more involved and supportive in their communities, so that they may live great lives, and empower their children to do the same.

From 2020-4 I sat as Global Chair of the Workplace Wellbeing Initiative at The Global Wellness Institute in Miami. Currently, from January 2025 onward, I have been Global Chair of Men's Wellbeing for GWI.

I am married to an outstanding woman, Lassen Aria Phoenix, a San Diego girl who spent many of her adult years in Seattle, Orlando and Salt Lake City. Between us we have 6 adult Children and seven grandchildren. We live in Australia but spend a lot of time in the US.

Contacting The Author

Wide Awake Wellness is my company. My Website is there for you to use. Please register for my newsletters so I can support you and your family to keep moving forward. We are currently changing our branding and soon we will be known as The Wellbeing Thought Leaders. It better describes all of our work.

All my articles are brief and to the point, so I promise not to labour you with intense and lengthy reads.

You will find the Website at https://wideawakewellness.com.au/.
Soon our Website will be https://wellbeingthoughtleaders.com

You can find me on **Instagram** at john.toomey and on **X** at @john.toomey.

The Gentlemen's Alliance
Our New Platform, thegentlemensalliance.com, will soon be active. It is an extensive education platform guiding men to robust and confident masculinity with courses for boys, adolescents, young men, new dads, new grandfathers, school teachers, sports coaches and employers.

On SubStack. My link is:
https://johntoomey.substack.com/publish/home

On LinkedIn:
https://www.linkedin.com/in/johntoomey-thoughtleader/

Podcast: Tune into my Podcast, the "Good Bloke, Not Woke!" Podcast where we discuss Confident Masculinity and Men's Wellbeing with some amazing guests. It is available on SubStack, Spotify, Rumble and YouTube.